The Duke  Duke's Desire

VOWS OF DESIRE

BOOK 2

A Steamy Historical Regency Romance Novel

by

Sienna Devereaux

RUBEDIA

PUBLISHING

Disclaimer & Copyright

Table of Contents

Letter from Sienna Devereaux

Hey, gorgeous!

I'm Sienna Devereaux, and I write romance for readers who love their dukes dirty and their heroines just a little bit dangerous. If it involves witty banter, a scandal in the making, or a candlelit moment that leads to utter ruin—I'm in!

I believe happily-ever-afters are earned through longing looks, smart choices, and at least one scene that makes you fan yourself.

By day, I chase my kids, bribe my husband into reading steamy drafts, and drink more tea than the ton at a Tuesday salon.

By night, I write from my slightly messy desk (and occasionally my bed), usually in yoga pants and always with tea.

If you're into witty women, wicked men, and slow-burns that explode, welcome. We're going to have so much fun!

Until our next delicious secret,

Sienna Devereaux

Chapter One

London was grey and wet. White fog swirled in the air, softened the edges of chimney pots, and settled into Miss Helena Darrow's auburn hair until each curl clung damp and stubborn about her temples. The chill reached through her spencer and muslin like a thief with deft fingers, prising into her bones despite the patter of her pulse.

She was abominably late to the appointment with Mr. Hart. Swearing under her breath—no true lady, her mother would have said, and yet her mother was not here to scold—Helena caught up fistfuls of her skirts and hitched them to her knees.

Yesterday's snow had melted and crusted over again in the night, leaving a treacherous mixture of ice glazed thin as spun sugar above ruts of black mud. It clutched at everything and had already seeped through her boots and stockings until her toes burned and then went numb.

For a heartbeat, she stood in the street's narrow throat between tall, soot-licked houses and considered turning back—simply not meeting Mr. Hart at all. The fog breathed in and out like some great animal, and she breathed with it, a steadying draught that tasted faintly of smoke and horse.

The weight of her choice settled about her shoulders like a heavy travelling cloak. It was not as though she truly wished to sign the contract Mr. Hart had drawn up.

Edmund waited in the hired hackney a few streets away, wrapped in his best coat and Meg's knitted scarf, his thin knees knocking when he was anxious, though he pretended they did not. She could go back to him, say she had changed her mind, and keep them both on the uncertain path they knew.

But she could not bear to leave matters as they were. Cowardice solved nothing; debt solved nothing.

She set her jaw and quickened her pace, picking her way over the uneven road with a recklessness born more of desperation than courage. A stitch lanced beneath her ribs. Her breath fogged white and vanished.

Hooves and wheels sliced the damp air—close. She turned her head just as a carriage shouldered through a sheet of standing water and flung it up in a glittering arc. The puddle slapped cold against her legs, heavy and shocking. She gasped. The carriage checked and came to a halt mere feet away, the horses blowing steam, leather harness creaking.

Heat of fury rose through the cold. Helena strode forward, heart thundering, and rapped her knuckles against the carriage door with more force than she intended. She meant to have an apology—at the very least—or coin for laundering. The door jerked open so sharply it nearly caught her cheek.

"Good morning, madam."

He descended with unhurried grace. Tall and austere, dark hair disciplined into order, eyes black and bright as polished jet. His greatcoat—broad of shoulder and perfectly brushed— gave him the air of a cantankerous crow who disliked being disturbed. He was immaculate. He was dry. An irrational part of Helena despised him for both when she was wet to the knees and splashed with London.

"Your driver has ruined my stockings and gown," she said, clipped as the frost.

"Unfortunate," he drawled, as if pronouncing on the weather.

"Is that all you have to say?"

One eyebrow climbed a fraction. "What would you have me say? Have you never walked in London? Mud will stain your hems. If such things vex you, you ought to consider taking a carriage."

Helena's fingers curled until the ache ran through her knuckles. A dozen scathing replies offered themselves and fled in the same instant, too sharp for prudence. But one escaped anyway, bright and reckless on her tongue.

"Perhaps if you looked where you were going instead of down your nose, sir, you might spare others your arrogance as well as your mud."

The words struck the air like flint on stone. His brows lifted, the faintest gleam of amusement—or warning—in his eyes. Heat rushed to her cheeks, mortification chasing fury.

She took a step to turn away, but her boot found a skin of invisible ice.

The world slipped. Street, horse, sky—all tilted backward—until a hard arm locked about her waist and held. It cost several beats of her startled heart to understand why she had not met the cobbles. The man had caught and steadied her, and though she stood upright again, he had not yet released his hold. The clean, restrained scent of his cologne—orange blossom and lavender—drowned the mould and gutter-reek for a breath.

She did not want his hands on her. Even disgraced, she remained the daughter of a gentleman. Yet a traitorous shiver, perilously like anticipation, skimmed her spine.

"Unhand me," she said, cool as she could make it.

He obeyed at once, an almost lazy condescension at the corner of his mouth. "There. I have spared your skirts from further ruin. We may call the account balanced."

"Balanced?"

"You were angered that my driver muddied your hem. I have prevented worse. Fair exchange. And now—if you would kindly be about your way. I have an appointment, and you have delayed me already."

Something in the unruffled superiority of him—his height, his immaculate coat, that idle certainty—unlocked a recklessness in Helena that was cousin to courage and kin to folly. Without taking her gaze from his face, she bent, scooped a palmful of slush and black London, and rose.

"Are you mad?" he demanded softly.

"Oh yes," she said. "Though not in the way you mean."

She pressed the mess to his lapel. He jerked back a fraction too late. The cool façade cracked, astonishment flaring cleanly. He could hardly have looked more scandalised had she struck him across the mouth.

"Now, all is fair."

Helena turned on her heel and strode off, skirts clutched high, breath shaking with cold and after-courage. Sensible fear arrived a few paces later. She had no notion who he was. What if he was vindictive? What if he followed?

She lengthened her stride until her calves burned and the ache in her side became a stitch proper. No steps came behind. She did not look back.

***

By the time she reached Mr. Hart's chambers, the fog had curled itself into the stairwell and clung to the brass rail. Helena's hands shook as she pushed open the door. A fair-haired, blue-eyed clerk sprang up so quickly his chair skittered. He stared outright for a beat—at her wind-snarled hair, her damp hem, the splash on her stocking—then recollected himself into a brisk bow.

"You must be Miss Darrow."

"Indeed."

A faint line wrote itself between his brows; the clock on the mantelshelf ticked pointedly. Helena sighed and set about the buttons of her spencer with stiff fingers. Heat bled from the small iron stove near the window; she longed to stand over it like a cat and thaw.

An inner door opened. A slight gentleman with neat auburn hair and clear blue eyes looked out, his glance sweeping her in one precise pass before returning to her face. "Miss Darrow! Please, come in. I am Nathaniel Hart, and I see you have met my clerk, Howell. You look chilled to the bone. Howell, take the lady's coat and bonnet."

Helena surrendered her things with gratitude and smoothed her hair to little avail. Her curls were temperamental at the best of times; once wetted, they preferred rebellion. Mr. Hart bowed and held the door, ushering her into a chamber book-lined and handsome in that modest professional way: sturdy desk, pigeon-holes, well-inked pens, a worn Turkey carpet, fire lively upon the hearth. The room smelled of paper and soap and a whisper of brandy.

"Will you take a glass?" Mr. Hart asked, pausing by a small stand upon which a decanter stood with two squat tumblers.

"Do you offer all your clients brandy?" she asked, mouth tugging despite herself.

"Usually," he said, and coloured faintly. "I seldom have dealings with ladies, Miss Darrow."

"Then I shall do you the honour of not confounding your custom." She accepted the glass. The spirit burned a clean path and left a little courage behind.

He took the chair opposite and studied her skirts with a scholar's attention. "That is lovely embroidery. Did you work it yourself?"

Helena lifted a brow, unsure why a solicitor wished to speak of needlework, though she preferred it to an admonition about the hour. "I did. Thank you."

"I am sadly ignorant of botany. Are they—?"

"Foxgloves," she supplied. "Digitalis. My favourite. Beautiful, and dangerous if mishandled. Not without medicinal use, however."

"Indeed?" He brightened. "I had the vague notion of it. Withering—Mr. Withering—wrote upon it, did he not?"

"He did," Helena said, and could not help herself: "His conclusions are interesting, though he is given to a sweeping tone."

Mr. Hart's mouth twitched. "The fault of many authors and some solicitors." He cleared his throat. "But I digress. Time is precious."

"It is," Helena agreed, and set her glass carefully upon a blotter. "I gather my groom-to-be has already left. Did he sign the contract?"

"He did not."

Her heart dropped like a stone down a well. "Why not?" The room tilted, just a little.

"Oh! You misunderstand me." Mr. Hart set down his own glass. "His Grace did not keep the appointment."

11

Cold crept into Helena's veins more efficiently than the fog ever had. "Do you know why?"

"I do not." He looked properly apologetic. "He has given me no indication that he wishes to withdraw, however, so I think it best we proceed. He may have been detained."

Detained. By indifference? By some new scandal? She could not decide how she felt. It was absurd to be wounded by a stranger's absence, and yet the slight stung. Perhaps she ought to be relieved; he could hardly scold her for tardiness when he had not come at all.

"Very well," she said, and kept her voice even.

Mr. Hart drew the contract from a leather portfolio and smoothed it flat with neat hands. "Would you like me to explain any part?"

Her gaze travelled the page. There was little mystery here: a marriage contract, a mutually advantageous arrangement between Lord Lucien Ashmore, Duke of Ravensgrave, and Miss Helena Darrow, late of Bloomsbury, with provisions for settlement of Mr. Darrow's debts, protection of certain effects belonging to his daughter, and a clause respecting the guardianship and education of Edmund Darrow.

"No," she said quietly. "I know what a marriage contract entails."

He offered pen and ink with a small, sincere smile. "Allow me to congratulate you, Miss Darrow. It is, if I may say so, an advantageous match—much desired by gentlewomen."

"Are you married, Mr. Hart?"

"No."

"That explains a great deal," Helena murmured, and then, because he looked wounded, softened the words. "An advantageous marriage has its appeal, certainly—but caution serves a woman better than enthusiasm. A title does not make a man worthy."

He regarded her with professional curiosity, as though she were a problem well-posed. "Are you hesitating?"

"A little," she said, truthfully.

The benefits were incontestable. She would not secure better: not with her father's name in the scandal sheets these two years running and her own visits to lecture halls whispered of with laughter that cut. This contract would settle the debts that pressed like stones upon her chest. It would head off any ugly contest over Edmund's guardianship. It would give him a future that did not begin with a closed door and end with a closed mouth.

"I would offer a word of advice," Mr. Hart ventured, tentative.

Helena's mouth went wry. "You are very good. I doubt clever words will ease my fears. Men discard women easily when they become inconvenient."

He stared as if she had uttered something in Greek, and perhaps she had for a solicitor. Helena signed before she could talk herself out of it. The scratch of the pen sounded very loud.

"It is done," she said.

Provided His Grace signed as well. If he did not, her choices narrowed to a pin-prick. She lifted the brandy again and finished it with more fortitude than grace; her eyes watered, and the heat ran like a small fire down her throat. Ill-advised— but if any moment warranted ill-advised comfort, it was consenting to wed a man she had never met, whose name the papers paired too readily with the word disgraced.

"Thank you for your time, Mr. Hart."

She rose. He opened his mouth—some polite felicitation trembling there—and she fled before it could alight.

In the outer office, Howell started, then hastened to fetch her bonnet and coat. The wool was blessedly dry against her chilled palms. Helena tied the ribbons beneath her chin with steadier fingers and stepped back into the London damp. The fog had thickened; lamps wore small halos; the world felt muffled and watchful.

She did not want Edmund waiting too near the office; discretion served as armour as surely as coin. Gossip bit hardest in winter when the ton scattered to their parks and parsonages, leaving space in the scandal sheets for smaller prey. A disgraced naturalist's daughter offered a neat mouthful.

She walked the agreed streets to the hackney, counting crossings to keep her mind from returning to the carriage and its intolerable gentleman. The horses tossed their heads as she approached; the driver touched his hat; she climbed inside.

Edmund started, his eyes—wide, green, and anxious—so like her own that for a moment she could not speak for tenderness. "Did you finish the business with the solicitor?"

"Yes," she said lightly. "He did not need me long."

Edmund did not know she had signed a marriage contract, and Helena meant to keep him innocent of it a little longer. He was ten: clever as a whip and soft as a peach, both at once. Besides, there remained the very real possibility His Grace would refuse to sign. After all, he had not kept the appointment.

"What shall we do now?" he asked, eager for orders, as if she were captain and he cabin-boy.

Helena pressed down the tide of doubt, drew him under her arm, and warmed his chilled hands between both of hers. "We shall go home and ask Meg for something warm and fortifying—posset if she is in a mood to be indulgent, chocolate if she is not. Then we will sit by the fire and read one of Mama's ghost stories."

Once, Meg had been Helena's nursemaid, then Edmund's; she had remained on through economies and embarrassments—one of the few servants Helena had kept, more from love than she would admit aloud. Meg claimed December belonged to ghosts because the nights came early and left late, and left room in between for listening.

Edmund brightened at once. "She always says December is best for ghost stories."

"So she does."

The hackney jolted into motion; the city unspooled—barrows and boys and a sweep of iron rail—like a ribbon tugged hand over hand.

A knot of longing drew tight beneath Helena's breastbone. Memory came in bright fragments: her mother's soft voice reading by candle's low flame; the scratch of a pen as she revised a sentence even while reading it aloud; her father's gentle smile when Helena corrected the Latin, his eyes glittering with a pride that was never loud enough to shame. He had been a progressive man, not threatened by a woman's mind, not afraid to stand beside his wife and daughter in rooms that did not want them.

Now both were gone, and it fell to Helena to gather the pieces they had left and build something that would not let Edmund fall through the cracks.

The hackney rattled on; the fog pressed its face to the glass and watched them pass.

She set her shoulders beneath the weight of the heavy cloak of choice. What she had done in Mr. Hart's office could not be undone. What remained was to carry it properly.

Outside, somewhere behind the veil of fog, a church bell counted the hour she had missed—and the hours left to make herself equal to what she had set in motion.

Chapter Two

Lucien stormed into the townhouse, his mood as dark as his title suggested. His arrival came hours later than anticipated—his entire day thrown into disarray by a mud-slinging madwoman in Clerkenwell.

Simon Richardson, Lucien's butler, bowed deeply. "Welcome home, Your Grace."

Lucien scowled.

Undeterred, Richardson took his coat and continued to smile in that polite, unflinching way that came of being entirely secure in one's position. He was an old man—the last relic of Lucien's father's household—spindly and pale, sparse white hair giving him a vaguely skeletal look. Yet he moved with the unhurried efficiency of long habit. The brass buttons on his coat were bright; his linen was immaculate; the hall itself bore the quiet order of his stewardship.

"Mr. Hart has sent correspondence for you."

"I am certain he has," Lucien said dryly. "I'll review it in my study. Bring a bottle of port."

"At once, Your Grace."

Relieved of his coat, Lucien tugged off his gloves and tossed them onto a nearby table. Emma, a maid lingering in the hall, darted forward and gathered them up with practiced speed.

"I shall tend to these, Your Grace."

He gave a curt nod and strode to his study, shutting the door with more force than necessary. His jaw tightened as his thoughts returned to the feisty young woman who had accosted him in the street. He had never witnessed such audacity.

In hindsight, perhaps he ought to have done something—pursued her, demanded recompense, insisted upon a magistrate. That might have been the proper course, ensuring she did not remain a menace to decent citizens. Truth told, astonishment had rooted him where he stood. He could only stare as that wild creature thundered away, skirts flying, eyes bright with temper.

Lucien dropped into the chair behind his desk and stared at the open ledger. The last thing he wished to see. Second only, perhaps, to the memory of that woman.

A knock sounded. "Enter," he barked.

Richardson appeared, bearing a sheaf of papers and a bottle of port. "As requested, Your Grace."

The butler uncorked the bottle, poured a generous measure into cut crystal, and set the glass before him with a deft turn of the wrist. He placed the bottle at Lucien's right hand—near enough to reach, far enough to discourage drinking from the neck.

"That will be all," Lucien said.

Richardson bowed. "As you wish, Your Grace."

When the door closed, Lucien exhaled and reached for the letters. He broke a wax seal and recognised Mr. Hart's tidy hand at once.

I am certain that some more pressing matter must have kept you from making our appointment this morning—

Lucien's scowl deepened; he set the letter aside. Hart was a fumbling man with little notion of how the *ton* operated, and that lack of polish never failed to irritate him. Ironic, then, that

Lucien had hired him precisely for that reason. Mr. Hart was competent and discreet—least likely, among London's solicitors, to gossip about a duke's private affairs.

The contract lay among the papers, neatly folded. Lucien opened it and scanned the clauses, the dense phrasing describing an arrangement as old as the peerage itself. At the bottom, *Helena Darrow* appeared in a delicate, looping hand.

That woman had agreed to be his wife.

He dipped his pen and signed beside her name, idly noting the contrast—her graceful loops against his spare, angular script. A faint smudge of ink caught at his forefinger; he wiped it away with a square of blotting paper. He had the vaguest recollection of the Darrow girl from childhood: pale and freckled, trailing after her eccentric father like a little shadow in lace and ribbons; a serious child, watchful. That was all.

The door burst open. Lady Honora stood framed upon the threshold like a Fury from the Underworld. Though nearly sixty, she remained stately and formidable, thick black hair arranged in meticulous curls, blue eyes sharp as cut glass. Her pale blue gown looked altogether too cheerful for her severe countenance.

"Aunt," Lucien said evenly, folding his hands atop the desk. "What a pleasant surprise."

"What have you done?" she demanded without preamble.

"You will have to be more specific."

"What is this I have heard about a marriage?"

Lucien smothered a spark of irritation. It was hardly a surprise she knew. If there was a scandal anywhere in Britain—no matter how carefully buried—Lady Honora would sniff it out.

"You did not consult me," she said.

"I was not obliged to."

Lady Honora inhaled sharply and pressed a gloved hand to her breast, as though mortally wronged. The scent of her lavender water drifted across the room, precise as her coiffure.

"It is not as though I have a wealth of options," Lucien said, voice low with irony. "The *ton* has long memories and delicate sensibilities. No lady of worth is eager to wed a man with scandal at his back, a burned estate, and blood on his name. But I still have a title, and titles have a way of buying obedience if not affection."

Her lip curled. "You still have much to offer."

Lucien scoffed. His first, cruel thought—*I am not Henry*—he bit back. Too callous, even for him.

"I am not in the habit of second-guessing my own decisions," he said, his voice low and final. "The match is made. The contract is signed."

"It is made of paper," Lady Honora countered sharply. "Paper burns—and it should. Women with tarnished reputations rarely remain in the background where they belong."

Lucien gave a short, dark laugh. "Then you and my wife will suit one another perfectly." He folded the contract with deliberate care and slid it into his breast pocket. "You both have a habit of ignoring the place society assigns you."

Lady Honora's eyes narrowed. "You mistake concern for insolence."

"And you mistake insolence for weakness," he said, rising. The quiet authority in his tone made the room still. "I will take some air. Alone."

Her mouth tightened. "Of course."

Lucien swept past, leaving her standing there, unwilling to waste another breath on the matter.

He crossed the tiled corridor and stepped into the cold. The townhouse gardens were more extensive than most in London—and nearly as neglected as his patience. After Henry's death, his father had lost all interest in the estate's upkeep. Pride had kept him from surrendering management to steadier hands.

Lucien entered the shuttered conservatory. Silence hung heavy, save for the faint leathery flutter of bats above the broken panes. Once, the place had been splendid—glass and paint and trained roses, his mother's careful hand everywhere. Now the glass was cracked, the paint flaked, and the air was thick with the sweet rot of old soil and dead leaves. Frost limned a fern's skeleton with delicate silver.

He crossed to the small table where he and Henry used to play chess. The board remained, dust-filmed, one rook toppled. Lucien's throat tightened.

"Sometimes," he murmured, "I wish it had been you instead of me. You would have worn the title better."

He had never been meant to be Duke of Ravensgrave. Everyone had known it would be Henry—the golden one, the charmer, the heir with a smile that could win anyone.

Lucien still remembered the rush to the duelling field and the sickening quiet that met him there. Henry's glove lay in the mud beside the pistol. The air had smelled of rain and blood and endings.

He drew a long breath and forced it out slowly. He had rules. One was not to linger on the past.

Yet Henry haunted every inch of the townhouse: the echo of his laughter in the stairwell, the remembered thud of his heel upon the landing, his ghost seated opposite at this battered board. Even the conservatory carried him—in the childish chalk marks still faint upon a table leg where they had once measured height against summer.

"And here I am," Lucien said under his breath, "speaking to ghosts and dying things. Fitting company for a man who outlived what mattered."

He brushed a hand along a ruined panel, tracing the faint painted petals of a pink rose. His chest tightened again. He was breaking another rule—thinking of her.

"You would hate this," he said under his breath.

Did he mean the ruin—the broken glass, the decay—or the marriage contract burning a hole in his pocket? His parents had been a love-match—rare, bright, and genuine. His own union was ink and duty.

He knew of Helena Darrow's reputation. He'd heard her name whispered often enough—usually behind fans or over brandy. *The naturalist's daughter, the one whose father lost his wits...* Her ruin had followed soon after. Some said she had driven a suitor to his death with her coldness.

At seven-and-twenty, she had been destined for spinsterhood. Desperate, but well-bred. That was all Lucien required: a wife who wanted stability, not sentiment.

If she was cold, so much the better. He had no warmth left to give.

He drew a slow breath, the air sharp with frost, and let it go between his teeth. "Well," he muttered, "what's done is done— better or worse."

He turned from the chess table without looking down, unwilling to face that toppled rook again. At the door, he paused. A draught slipped through the broken panes and ruffled his hair; the night beyond smelled of iron and frost.

"Forgive me or don't," he said under his breath. "It changes nothing. I'll do what must be done."

He stepped into the moonlit garden, boots crunching over frost. The memory of that wild woman who'd dared to fling mud at him pulled a low sound from his throat—half a laugh, half a growl.

Reckless, infuriating creature. The thought of marrying *her* instead of the prim Miss Darrow almost made him laugh. Lady Honora would likely faint—or draw a pistol.

Perhaps his aunt was right. The spinster might not remain meek and quiet—but he could certainly marry worse.

Chapter Three

Ravensgrave Hall, the ancestral seat of the Duke of Ravensgrave, rose from the moors like a monument to death. The house was all black stone and frost-laced windows.

Skeletal remnants of grass and flowers lay strewn along the path like fallen soldiers. Doubtless, some had fallen prey to winter, but studying the dilapidated estate, Helena found it difficult to believe that anything had ever grown here at all.

Even the wind seemed to pass it by in a hurry, as though unwilling to linger.

She frowned, letting her sharp gaze travel over the property. His Grace had signed the contract and wasted no time in demanding she come to Yorkshire for the wedding. She supposed she ought to be relieved; the journey from London had supplied ample time to think—too much time, perhaps.

She did not know this man. She knew only whispers—the ruin of his estate, the shadows on his name—and the uneasy truth that soon she would belong to him.

Still, for no reason she could name, her mind flickered back to the stranger who had drenched her in mud days ago—the hard line of his jaw, the steel in his voice. She pushed the thought aside. That man, at least, she would never see again.

"Are we going there?"

At Edmund's sleepy voice, Helena returned to the hired hackney. Her brother sat on the floor, swinging his legs, his cap tilted over one ear in a manner that always made her heart ache.

"We are," she said. "Meg is going to gain us entrance."

The night before, while Edmund slept against her shoulder, Helena and Meg had bent close beneath the weak lamp of the coach. Meg's fingertip traced a plan on the fogged glass—gate, kitchen yard, narrow stair, nursery.

We hide him there, her look said, *until we know what sort of man he is.*

Helena's throat tightened. The duke's solicitor had been explicit: the marriage would proceed only on the understanding that Edmund be sent to a school in the north— respectable, distant, and safely out of her keeping. *His Grace will not have the boy under his roof,* Mr. Hart had said, eyes darting from her face to the contract as though ashamed of the clause he recited.

Helena had signed anyway. What choice had she? But she could no more send Edmund away than she could tear out her own heart. She would keep him close until she learned whether the Duke of Ravensgrave was the kind of man who honoured such terms—or the kind who could be made to forget them.

Meg had agreed and gone to bribe the groundskeeper with the last of Helena's money. It had not been much. She had felt each shilling part from her palm like a tooth pulled.

If all went well, the groundskeeper would help them slip Edmund through a servants' entrance and into some place where he might remain hidden.

Even though it was late, Helena could see the estate was in disrepair. Parts of Ravensgrave Hall appeared scorched or otherwise grievously damaged, as if the fire had licked its way along corridors and simply...stopped.

After what felt like an eternity, Meg returned. She was a robust woman—tall, broad-shouldered, of impressive girth. Her golden hair and blue eyes were lovely; when Helena was little, she had declared Meg an angel on the strength of that face alone. Her parents had laughed, and Meg had pretended to be offended and then fed Helena honey-bread.

"I know where to go," Meg said, cheeks pink from the cold. "Our man is not overburdened with scruples, thank Heaven."

"Splendid," Helena answered. "Come along, Edmund."

Meg led them by a rough path behind Ravensgrave. The ground was uneven; frost crackled beneath their feet. Remembering Clerkenwell, Helena took considerably more care than she might have done a week ago, testing each patch with the toe of her boot before committing her weight. The moor stretched away on every side, a long sweep of pewter and shadow; somewhere a curlew called, thin and mournful.

"A few years ago Ravensgrave Hall caught fire," Meg said quietly, as if the house might overhear.

"I suspected as much."

"Yes. His Grace has not repaired the worst of it, and the staff seldom goes into that part of the house. Fortunately for us, there is an old nursery. Somewhat ragged, but it will be... adequate."

Guilt pricked. Edmund had never asked for much—never the new toy in a shop window, never sweetmeats when they passed a confectioner. He was an astute child and had learned far too early the reality of their situation. He watched her when he thought she did not see, counting her coins with his eyes.

"Do you see that light?" Meg asked. "Our groundskeeper left a lantern to guide us."

At last, they reached a door, which Meg heaved open. The hinges creaked ominously, a long, thin wail. Moonlight fell upon a corridor draped in cobwebs, dust veiling the skirting like gauze. Helena took up the lantern and lifted it high; the little flame flickered and threw uneasy shadows. The air smelled of cold stone and old smoke. It did nothing to make the interior of Ravensgrave more appealing.

"Where from here?" Helena asked.

"We shall come to a stair," Meg said. "Turn left at the top—that is the east wing. The nursery is on the left side of the corridor. Our man could not recall precisely where but says we shall not miss it."

"We shall see."

They set out through the dark interior, which put Helena rather in mind of a tomb. Their footsteps made soft, hollow sounds. She shivered, recalling one of her mother's stories about an abandoned manor filled with revenants—the restless dead who rose by moonlight to trouble the living. It had been meant as a lark; tonight, it felt like a warning. They reached the stair and took the left-hand passage. Long scorch marks marred the stone like grasping fingers. Here and there, the black had bubbled with heat and then cooled into a rippled gloss.

"This is scary," Edmund whispered, clutching her skirts.

It was. Helena made herself smile. "Only because it is night. Once Meg has you snug in the nursery, it will not seem so dreadful. And when daylight comes, I daresay the sun must shine exquisitely on all this black stone."

The lies fell easily. She thanked God, silently, for the small spark of her mother's gift. She would make a fair world for him out of words if she could not buy him one.

"Here," Meg breathed.

She had halted by an open doorway. The door itself was long gone. Helena held the lantern into the room. A rusted hobbyhorse did, indeed, mark it a nursery. Half the chamber bore the stains of fire; the other half kept a ragged fringe of wallpaper printed with stags, and a cracked hearth with a little fan of ash beneath the grate as if it still remembered flame.

Helena went to the bed and pressed the mattress with care. Ancient, but sound enough. It would do for a few days.

"I brought clean linens," Meg said, already shaking them out with businesslike vigour. "If we lay them on the bed, it will not be so bad. We can light a small fire. With everyone abed, it will pass unnoticed."

Meg did her best to make the place cheerful: a folded blanket at the foot; Edmund's book placed square upon the little table; his wooden soldier stood at attention on the sill, keeping guard against the dark. It did not look fit for anyone—least of all a child—but what choice had they?

Helena could not present her brother to this stranger until she knew what sort of man he was.

"It will only be a few days," she murmured.

She was reassuring herself as much as Edmund.

"Yes," Meg said. "I shall pose as your maid. No one will question it. When you do not need me, I will come to Edmund, and we shall make such mischief here. We shall have a kingdom of our own in the east wing, see if we do not."

Helena nodded. "I only wish I were not engaged upon business, so I might join you."

"Do you truly have to do business?" Edmund asked. "It is all rather strange, sister."

"I know," Helena said.

"Why must I hide?"

"Because I must be certain you will be safe." She kissed his hair. "You may not understand now, but you shall."

"Yes," Meg added, softening. "You are fortunate in your sister's devotion. Come—bed."

Edmund frowned but did not argue. Some of the tightness left Helena's shoulders when his lashes finally lowered. She stood a moment longer, watching the slow rise and fall of his breath.

In the morning, she would stage her arrival at Ravensgrave, meet her groom, and *perhaps*... discover he was not as monstrous as his home.

***

Late in the morning, Helena approached the front gate. She had made certain her appearance was immaculate, her cloak and gown free of the dust and cobwebs from the ruined wing. The air had a bright, brittle feel; the moor looked clean-washed beneath a pale sun. A footman awaited her, his livery neat, his expression carefully empty.

"Good morning," she said. "I am Helena Darrow. His Grace is expecting me."

"So he is." The answer came in a sonorous, masculine voice.

Not the footman. Helena's head snapped toward the speaker—and she gasped so sharply her chest ached. The cantankerous raven himself.

The man from Clerkenwell.

He froze.

Helena wished the earth would open and swallow her to the frozen floor of Hell.

He cleared his throat.

Another silence.

The footman looked between them, uneasy. "Shall I open the gate for her, Your Grace?"

His Grace. *That* man.

Helena's mind said *run*, but her body refused to move. Already, the marriage seemed doomed. The duke was worse than she'd imagined—taller by daylight, broader through the shoulders, his eyes as hard and dark as obsidian.

"No," he said, voice low and even. "I'll see to it myself. Leave us."

The footman bowed and vanished, leaving Helena alone with him—the man she'd splattered with mud, the man who held her future in his gloved hands.

He came closer to the bars, that faint, predatory half-smile curling his mouth. "No sharp words today? No lecture on civility?"

She lifted her chin. "I was only startled to discover my husband-to-be is such a rude and disrespectful man."

His eyes narrowed slightly, the smile deepening. "You mistake indifference for rudeness. I don't waste courtesy on strangers who throw mud."

"Your driver ruined my gown."

"And you ruined my morning." His voice was quiet, but there was steel beneath it. "It seems we're even."

"The situations are not the same."

"They are precisely the same," she said, heat rising to her cheeks. "And if we're comparing offenses, you didn't even bother to attend your own appointment with Mr. Hart."

"I don't answer to solicitors—or to women I haven't married," he said smoothly. "I was not about to sit in an office reeking of ink and desperation while covered in mud."

Helena bristled. "I cannot imagine why you would require a marriage of convenience. Surely women must be queuing for the pleasure of your company."

"Women," he said with a faint shrug, "prefer charm. I prefer silence."

Her temper sparked. "How fortunate for you, then, that I have no wish to chatter."

"Fortunate indeed." His gaze held hers, deliberate and unflinching.

"You're very bold for a woman outside the gate," he said softly. "Now, Miss Darrow, suppose I don't open this gate. Would you walk back to London—or stand here all day pretending you aren't shivering?"

She drew breath for another fierce answer—and stopped. She needed to marry this man. For Edmund's sake, she must.

"I apologise for the slight in Clerkenwell," she said, the words tight.

"Good," he said, almost gently. "But not enough."

Her fingers tightened on the iron. "I apologise, Your Grace."

His smile deepened. He shook his head. "Hardly better."

"I am cold," she snapped, hands curling about the bars. "You are a duke. This is childish—and beneath you."

A black-haired woman in Paris green slipped from the door of Ravensgrave. Even at a distance, she cut a striking figure. "And is this Miss Darrow?" she asked.

Something swift and hot flickered in His Grace's eyes, too brief for Helena to read. He turned slightly. "My aunt, Lady Honora."

Helena curtsied—and belatedly realised she ought to have curtsied to him as well.

Lady Honora's smile was as poisonous as belladonna. "Miss Darrow. As expected."

The duke unlocked the gate and gave Helena a warning look. "I invited my aunt to join us for refreshments. You must be famished after such a journey."

His tone had softened, polished. The abrupt change unsettled her more than the mockery had. Moments ago, he'd looked ready to leave her in the cold; now he played the courteous host, his words measured and genteel.

Helena forced a small, polite smile. It wasn't kindness—of that she was certain. It was a performance. Whatever this man wished her to believe, she would be wise to remember the mud, the smirk, and the gate that had stayed locked until he'd decided to open it.

"Indeed, I am," Helena said, willing her voice steady.

He locked the gate behind them. They crossed the court and entered the house. The great hall opened in lavish contrast to the gate-yard: gleaming rosewood, rugs woven in scarlet and gold, tapestries of medieval hunts. To one side, a gilded staircase cut through the black stone with startling elegance. The air smelled faintly of beeswax and old smoke, as if the fire had left its ghost behind.

The drawing-room was equally handsome. Large windows overlooked the moors; morning light softened the severity of the dark walls. Lady Honora took a chair, leaving the settee to Helena. She sat at one end. After a measured pause, His Grace sat at the other.

They were a more than respectable distance apart.

"Tea," Lady Honora snapped to a fair-haired parlour-maid, who hastened to obey.

"We should discuss the finer points of our marriage," His Grace said. A beat. "If we are married."

Helena inclined her head. She ached for solitude to think. It seemed impossible to tie herself to this detestable man. She ought to leave at once, fetch Edmund, and—

Edmund. If she married, she could secure his future. She pictured his lashes on his cheek, the wooden soldier on the windowsill, standing guard.

"Your title will not be used until marriage," Lady Honora said. "I trust you have no objection."

Wouldn't that have been true in any case? Helena forbore argument. Greater concerns pressed: *was* she going to do this?

"And I am not inclined to use titles at Ravensgrave," the duke added, as if stating a household rule. His voice held the calm certainty of a man accustomed to obedience.

To Helena, it sounded less a preference than a decree — as if he were drawing a line through every rule of polite society and daring them to cross it.

"Excuse me?" Lady Honora asked.

"In formal rooms, certainly. Not in my house."

Lady Honora sighed. "My dear nephew—"

"I know what you will say," he cut in, voice even as a blade laid flat. "Let us not quarrel."

The calm steel under his tone was familiar to Helena already. If she must endure this man, perhaps his aunt might prove an ally.

Or not. Although Helena had only just met her, Lady Honora managed to be as condescending as her nephew—if not more.

"I am not a particularly formal man, Miss Darrow," he said.

The maid returned with the tray and spared Helena the necessity of answering. In another circumstance, she would have been relieved to learn her groom was not a stickler for ceremony; she knew very little of the *ton* and doubted she knew all that was required of a duchess. A husband tolerant of blunders would have been a blessing.

If only the husband were not *him*.

As Helena took her tea, she thought of Meg and Edmund in the hidden nursery. Edmund needed her. Whether she liked the duke or not, she must marry him.

Her spoon clinked against porcelain. Lady Honora's mouth pinched. Helena winced inwardly and lifted the cup to scent the brew.

Valerian. She blinked. An unusual choice for guests— earthy, calming, with a bitter little edge beneath.

"Is there a problem?" His Grace asked.

Not displeased—merely curious. His eyes were on her hands, not her face.

"I am surprised it is valerian root. Uncommon."

"It is my favourite."

"If we are married, I suppose I shall develop a liking for it," Helena said. "Your Grace."

Favourite blend or not, it remained an odd choice for company. She took a careful sip.

Chapter Four

The Ravensgrave chapel was as cold and sombre as the bargain that had brought Helena to its door.

She was damp from the light rain, but her gown had been chosen with care. From experience, Helena knew the pale brown dye would not bleed easily, even in the wet.

The garment was modest, simple, and neatly pressed. She had endeavoured to make it more suitable for so momentous an occasion, embroidering clusters of lilac forget-me-nots about the waist and hem. The little flowers steadied her; stitch by stitch, she had told herself a story about courage.

She was securing Edmund's future with this marriage. Helena pushed open the black iron gate, her boots clicking sharply against the stone path that led to the small, dark chapel.

The building was grey and dismal, the rose window dulled by the stormy light. Rain threaded from the gutters in fine, silver strands. She pulled open the dark wooden door; cold air breathed out to meet her.

A delighted cry split the air, and Helena started. For a second, her senses were overwhelmed by English lavender and a sweep of night-black hair. "You are beautiful!" a young, feminine voice exclaimed. "It is so wonderful to meet you!"

Without warning, arms wrapped around her. Helena stiffened, more startled than anything else. Beautiful.

She had never been a great beauty.

"Ch-charmed," Helena managed. "Who are you?"

The dark-haired woman released her and held her at arm's length. She looked nearly Helena's age, with a delicate, elfin face and sly hazel eyes. "I am Beatrice Ashmore. His Grace is my cousin."

"Lady Beatrice Ashmore?" Helena asked hesitantly.

"Oh! Yes—Lady Beatrice," she said, laughing at herself. "You may call me Beatrice, though. I imagine we shall be great friends."

Helena stared. Part of her was deeply confused; surely proper ladies did not behave so. She almost wondered if this were a cruel jest—*let us make sport of the naturalist's daughter*—but Beatrice's enthusiasm seemed so sincere that Helena felt her doubts melt in the warmth of that smile.

"Yes," Helena said. "I think so."

"Shall I make introductions?" Beatrice asked, linking her arm with Helena's. "It will keep me from chattering at you until you faint."

Helena's gaze swept the other occupants. Her breath caught; she found her groom.

The cantankerous raven. He looked perfectly at home in the colourless chapel—tall against the grey, severe as the stone itself.

Her heart hammered so violently it seemed to echo in her skull. His eyes met hers for a heartbeat. He turned and spoke to the vicar, too low for her to catch the words. His expression gave her nothing—only that cool, measuring calm she had already come to hate.

Fear seized her like claws, his earlier words playing in her head as if remembered music. *If we are married*, he had said.

37

Had he changed his mind? Was he calling it off? Had one ill-judged act ruined Edmund's future? *Could she still salvage this?*

"My aunt, Lady Honora, was regrettably unable to join us," Beatrice was saying.

It took all of Helena's will to hear her. Was there a deeper meaning? *Unable*, or had Lady Honora chosen not to attend on principle? It was plain the lady loathed her.

It mattered little. If Lady Honora was absent, she could not interrupt.

"This is Mr. Peter Langford, the estate's steward," Beatrice said, guiding her forward.

Mr. Langford bowed deeply. He looked near forty and carried his years well—brown hair like oak leaves, eyes blue as cornflowers, a steadiness about the mouth that suggested competence rather than charm.

"A pleasure, Miss Darrow."

"Likewise," she said, grateful for the ordinary civility of it.

With undimmed eagerness, Beatrice brought Helena to her groom. His Grace's expression was unreadable. Helena searched for a scrap of warmth and found none. He did not offer his arm; she climbed the steps alone. They faced one another. The smell of cold stone and wet wool wrapped about them both.

Helena withheld a sigh. She was unsurprised to find him so cold, but the whole ceremony felt... vaguely uncomfortable. It was like stepping onto a stage where everyone knew their lines except the heroine.

"Shall we begin?" the vicar asked brightly, adjusting his spectacles with hands stained faintly with ink.

"Yes," the duke said.

The vicar cleared his throat and nearly fell into a coughing fit that echoed off the rafters. "Dearly beloved, we are gathered together here in the sight of God, and in the face of this congregation, to join together this man and this woman in holy matrimony, which—unto us—*is* the mystical union—"

Helena frowned, fairly certain he had stumbled and missed a line, but said nothing. Neither did anyone else. She supposed it hardly mattered. The contract was signed; the words were only the ribbon tied about a box already sealed.

No one pretended the marriage was founded on love and mutual respect. Why should it matter if the vicar made a few errors? This was formality.

As he continued, Helena's thoughts drifted. Droplets gathered and fell from the ceiling; small tongues of green moss crept between stones. A draught found the hem of her gown and worried at the embroidery as if to lift the forget-me-nots free.

"I will," His Grace said.

A lump rose in Helena's throat. They had reached that part already. He had agreed to marry her. She had only to repeat the words, and she would be the Duchess of Ravensgrave.

Edmund would have a future. She saw, as clearly as if he stood beside her, his lashes dark upon his cheek as he slept, the wooden soldier keeping guard upon the sill of the ruined nursery. *Hold fast,* she told herself. *For him.*

"Helena Rose Darrow," intoned the vicar, "wilt thou have this man to thy lawfully wedded husband, to live together after God's ordinance in the holy estate of matrimony? Wilt thou obey him, and serve him, love, honour, and keep him, in sickness and in health, and, forsaking all others, keep thee only unto him, so long as ye both shall live?"

Obey him. Of all the words, those gave her pause. She swallowed. She had found it pitiable that Mr. Hart failed to grasp the dangers marriage posed to women; and yet was she not more pitiable, knowing those dangers and still choosing to wed?

"This is where you speak," the vicar prompted gently. "Miss Darrow."

He meant to be kind—he thought nerves had overcome her. Somewhere behind her, Beatrice's gloved fingers tightened in quick encouragement.

His Grace's gaze seemed to sharpen, as if he could hear the machinery of her fear turning.

"I do," Helena rasped. "I will."

A tomb creaked shut in her mind. It was done. She had agreed to her own imprisonment—as this man's wife and duchess.

A ring was offered. Helena did not resist as His Grace slipped it onto her finger. The band of gleaming gold made the loveliest shackle. The weight was slight, and yet it altered the balance of her hand.

This is your own thought, she chastised herself. *You cannot complain when you have done this with full awareness of what it means.*

Even knowing she authored her own fate, she could not muster enthusiasm when the vicar declared her a married woman. The words struck the air and fell heavy; no bell rang, no cheer rose—only the quiet of rain and breath.

"I would prefer that we not," Helena said softly, though her voice lacked its usual steel.

The duke turned his head toward her, slow and deliberate. The flicker of a smile ghosted his mouth—not amusement, not kindness, but something that warned. "You would prefer?" he echoed, voice pitched low enough that it seemed to vibrate through her bones.

He moved closer, his shadow falling across her gown, the faint scent of spice and smoke curling in the cold air between them. "A pity," he murmured, "for it is customary all the same."

Before she could draw breath to argue, his hand caught hers—firm, gloved fingers closing around her wrist. He did not tug, merely held her still. His thumb pressed once against the delicate beat beneath her skin, as though testing how fast her heart ran. Then he lowered his head and brushed his mouth across her knuckles—unhurried, certain, a dark promise masquerading as courtesy.

When he lifted his head, his eyes held hers—dark, unreadable, faintly amused, as though daring her to flinch. "There," he said softly. "Custom satisfied."

Beatrice gave a small, nervous laugh. "Beautiful," she whispered again, though even she sounded unconvinced.

Helena could only stare at him.

"Convey my thanks to the vicar," the duke said, voice low, already turning to the practicalities.

His Grace cleared his throat and offered his arm. Heat rose to Helena's face. She refused it and swept past him, making all haste to the chapel doors. A carriage waited. A footman hastened forward, but Helena tore open the door before he could touch the latch. She gathered her skirts and lighted into

41

the carriage. The leather seat was cold; the glass had filmed with rain.

By the time her *husband* joined her, she had already been seated on the cushioned bench for several minutes. His coat carried the faint, clean scent of that cologne she remembered only as *a stranger's*. "Do not do that again," Helena said. "Ever."

He settled opposite and gave no answer—only the faintest smile, as if he fully intended to test the boundary again when it pleased him. He knocked once on the roof; the carriage jolted forward. Outside, the chapel dwindled into grey.

Obey him rang in Helena's ears. She wrapped her arms about herself and turned to the window. It was the only way to keep from coming apart.

When the glass blurred, she told herself it was the rain.

Chapter Five

The next morning, Lucien entered the dining hall to find his wife already there. She was dressed in a simple blue gown, the bodice and sleeves embroidered with delicate sprays of white and green flowers.

A proper duchess would never wear something so plain. Still, it suited her. She sat, poised and composed, her expression unreadable.

Breakfast would not be ready for some time yet, but already she had taken a cup of tea, its colour dark and seemingly undiluted by either sugar or milk.

He took his usual seat, aware of her eyes following his every movement. "I suppose we ought to discuss our arrangement more thoroughly now that we are wed, Miss—" He broke off. "I cannot call you Miss Darrow."

"Given that I am no longer Miss Darrow, I suppose not."

Lucien wondered if she woke every morning with the personal aim of being as contrary as possible.

"Now, what do I call you?" he mused.

"Helena."

He frowned, vaguely unsettled. It was a perfectly reasonable request from his wife, yet he found himself wanting to deny it. Calling her *Helena* felt too intimate.

"Only at Ravensgrave," he said at last. "Everywhere else, you will be *my lady* and *Her Grace*. Sometimes, *my wife*."

"Fine," she said. "I will address you in the same manner."

That was a start.

"I need a wife who is discreet," he said. "Quiet and pleasing to the eye."

"Charming," she said dryly.

He scowled, voice low. "You speak like a woman who has never been taught the cost of defiance. I care little for society's rules, but in this house, mine are the only ones that matter—and you will learn them soon enough."

"And yet you married me still, despite all my flaws."

His gaze hardened. "I did. And you might consider showing a measure of gratitude instead of testing the limits of my tolerance. There will be no more public scenes. Not while you bear my name."

Helena smiled thinly. "Thank you for so very clearly defining the terms of my captivity."

Before Lucien could retort, his aunt entered. "My dear nephew. Helena. Good morning."

"Good morning," Lucien said.

Helena echoed his sentiments and took a sip of tea, her sly eyes gleaming over the rim of her cup.

"Your composure is a sight to behold, Helena," Lady Honora said as she seated herself at the table.

"That is kind of you to observe, my lady," Helena said.

"It is."

If the atmosphere had not been so tense between them all, Lucien might have laughed at the absurdity of their situation. They were seated in the dining hall well before breakfast would be ready. He imagined the staff had already noticed, and the cook was likely in a frenzy, hastening the dishes all the more quickly.

"Some women adapt to households with startling speed," Lady Honora continued. "We shall see if you are such a woman, Helena."

"Indeed," she said.

Lucien glanced between the two of them. He felt as though Helena and his aunt were engaged in some private war, and he had not the faintest idea which of them would emerge victorious.

***

When the two of them shared a room, it was like watching a tempest battle an earthquake, and he was no fool to stand between them.

He poured himself a measure of brandy before settling behind the desk. When his temper was frayed, he turned to Marcus Aurelius. The precision of Latin steadied him; its logic reminded him that even fury could be ordered, mastered, bent to will.

He traced the spine of the old volume with a calloused thumb. Henry had never cared for languages; they had been Lucien's one arena of triumph.

Yet the words blurred before his eyes. He closed the book with a decisive snap that cracked the silence.

It was impossible to think on philosophy when his mind kept returning to her. *Helena.* Not what he had expected in a wife, much less a duchess. She refused to simper or charm. She challenged, provoked—met him blow for blow.

He found himself smirking despite it.

She covered me in mud.

The memory no longer stung; it almost pleased him. It had taken nerve to defy a duke in the middle of London.

Perhaps that was what unsettled him most—her nerve. Most women curtsied and yielded. She did neither. She met his eyes as if she saw something in him worth fighting.

He leaned back in his chair, the leather creaking under his weight. "Brazen little hellcat," he muttered, half amused, half admiring.

His aunt had warned him she would be trouble. For once, the woman was right.

He stood and stretched, broad shoulders pulling tight against his shirt.

If he could not lose himself in the order of Latin, then he would find order elsewhere. Work. Control. Anything to quiet his thoughts.

He left Marcus Aurelius on the desk and strode out. He left his study and descended the stairs. He pushed open the door and entered the gardens.

The brisk winter wind left him nearly breathless. He considered returning for his coat but chose instead to endure the frigid air.

He tucked his hands into his pockets and followed the familiar path. Overnight, snow had fallen. It lingered still in deep, soft-looking crests of white, but the walk had been cleared already. Perhaps that was the work of the gardener, who knew of his fondness for walking the grounds.

A better man might have asked Helena to join him. She was a naturalist's daughter, after all. He did not know if she shared her father's interest in botany, but the embroidered flowers on

46

her gowns seemed to indicate some interest in plant-life. It must have taken hours to work all that.

He passed Thomas, the gardener, who bowed deeply. "Your Grace!" he exclaimed, sounding surprised.

Lucien gave a small, acknowledging nod. "Thank you for clearing the path for me."

"It is my pleasure, but I must confess I did not clear the path for you. Her Grace came to the gardens a couple of days ago and mentioned wishing to explore them further."

When had Helena done that? Lucien sheepishly rubbed the back of his neck, for he ought to have known where his wife went about the estate.

"In that case, thank you for looking out for my wife."

My wife. The words sounded heavier than he'd meant them. Possessive. Final. He frowned, unsettled by how naturally they had left his mouth. Why *my wife*, and not *Helena*? A small thing, yet it spoke of claim rather than convenience.

She was his wife, yes—but he preferred not to think of her in any way that implied attachment. He shoved his hands into his coat pockets and continued down the path, long strides cutting through the cold air. He should have laid out her boundaries more plainly, made her understand the order of his house and the limits of his tolerance. Even after a single day of marriage, he could feel her upending his routines, needling at his composure.

He reached the conservatory and stopped short. The half-broken door stood ajar, shuddering faintly in the wind. He narrowed his eyes. He had locked that door himself.

Lucien entered, the air sharp with the scent of frost and damp earth. Morning light streamed through the shattered panes, painting his breath in silver mist. He stilled, gaze sweeping over the ruin until it caught—then hardened.

The ivy. Someone had cut it back. The thick vines that had strangled his mother's lilies lay hacked and curling across the floor like slain serpents.

His shoulders went rigid. Two strides took him to the wall. He brushed his fingers over the fresh cuts, his jaw locking tight.

Someone is changing Ravensgrave.

Without my leave. Without my word.

The thought coiled through him like heat meeting steel. This house was his—every stone, every shadow. No one touched it without permission.

His gaze caught on the bench nearby. A trowel rested there, gleaming clean, unused to the grime of Ravensgrave's earth. He picked it up, turning it in his hand. Not one of his tools. Not one of his men's.

Cold steadiness replaced the first flare of anger. Only one person in this cursed house would dare make alterations as if she owned the place.

He exhaled slowly through his nose, the trowel biting cold against his palm. "Of course," he muttered. "Her."

The word was half curse, half challenge.

He took the trowel with him, fury tangling inside him. He knew it was irrational to be so angry, but he could not help it.

Ravensgrave was his home, and he would decide what changes were made to it. If he let her prune the vines without comment, Helena would want to make more changes. And more.

And he could not bear that. Any alterations at Ravensgrave must be handled delicately, with his oversight, because there were—

There were so many ghosts etched into the stone and wood and glass of Ravensgrave, and he must ensure they were not forgotten.

As he came up the path, he met the gardener again. "Thomas," Lucien said, his tone clipped, "have you made any changes in the conservatory?"

The man straightened at once. "No, Your Grace. I have not gone near the conservatory, per your orders."

Lucien studied him in silence for a moment—long enough that Thomas shifted his weight, visibly uneasy beneath the duke's gaze. "And you are certain," Lucien said at last, "that no one else has been sent to work there? No housemaids with too much curiosity? No idle hands wandering where they should not?"

"N-no, Your Grace. I suppose the housekeeper would know, but I have not seen anyone else in the gardens."

Lucien's eyes narrowed, though his expression remained calm. "Good. See that it stays that way."

"Yes, Your Grace."

He inclined his head once—more dismissal than gratitude. "That will be all."

As he entered the manor, he became aware of just how cold he had been in the garden. Sighing, he climbed the stairs and returned to his study. He stowed the trowel in the drawer of his desk and poured himself a glass of brandy.

"Now, what do I do?" he muttered.

His first impulse was to confront her. To drag her into his study and demand an explanation until she understood what Ravensgrave meant to him.

But he stopped himself.

It was not mercy that held him—it was control.

Anger, he had learned, was a weapon best kept sheathed until it struck clean.

He exhaled through his nose, the sound low, deliberate. She had not torn the conservatory apart; she had merely trimmed what any gardener might have. Still, the fact that she had done it without his leave burned like a brand. A wife who moved through his domain as if it were her own—he would have to decide whether to break that habit or bend it to his purpose.

He planted both palms on the desk, the muscles in his forearms taut beneath his sleeves. He would wait. He would watch her a little longer before making his move. He had no desire to lash out in temper; cruelty was easy, but control—that was power.

And Helena Darrow was precisely the sort of woman who would test a man's power to its limit.

He took up his glass and drank. "Henry would have had her writing sonnets by now," he muttered. "He always did know how to charm the defiant ones."

The brandy burned down his throat. He stared into the amber liquid, jaw flexing.

Lucien lowered the glass slowly. The ache in his chest pressed harder, familiar, unwanted. If he had been half a step faster that day, his brother might still be alive.

He ground his teeth, forcing the thought back where it belonged—in the dark, locked place where he kept all the things he could not afford to feel.

And still his mind betrayed him, circling back to her.

Helena Darrow, with her stubborn chin and sharp tongue, the woman who dared cut into his house without leave.

Chapter Six

Helena hugged Edmund tightly, desperate to keep herself from falling to pieces. Edmund and Meg were still staying in the nursery, waiting for Helena to make her determination about His Grace's character. Lucien's character, rather.

She had said that she would call him that.

"How long are we going to remain here?" Edmund asked.

"Just a little longer," Helena said. "I promise."

She looked at Meg, whose eyes shone with questions for which Helena was uncertain she had answers.

"But we are enjoying ourselves very much!" Meg exclaimed. "We have been sketching the room, and I have been reading your father's journals."

Helena suspected the reassurance was for her benefit as much as for Edmund.

"I will return soon," Helena said, forcing a smile. "Perhaps I can stay a little longer when I do."

Edmund dropped his arms and stared at her, his face so innocent and believing that Helena's heart clenched. She needed to take Edmund from this dreadful room as quickly as she possibly could.

Helena slipped away from the east wing. "Helena."

Lady Honora's voice brought her up short. Helena spun, pulse jumping.

"What are you doing?" Lady Honora asked.

"Looking," Helena said. "I was never offered a tour of Ravensgrave. I thought to explore."

With a jolt of dread, she realised that she might have misspoken. She needed Edmund to remain hidden, and she hoped that Lady Honora would not thoughtfully offer a tour of the grounds.

"You do not want to wander that way," Lady Honora said. "That entire wing is ruined."

There was no offer for a tour. Helena had overestimated Lady Honora's charity.

"I did not know," Helena said. "How did that happen?"

"That is of no concern to you. Come. We should discuss some things."

Helena would have loved to refuse, but she did not wish to arouse suspicion by declining to speak with Lady Honora.

"Of course," Helena said.

She followed Lady Honora to the drawing room, Helena's spirits lifting a little when she saw that Beatrice was also present. Seeing her, the young woman smiled brightly. "Your Grace, we meet again."

"There is no need to call her *Your Grace*," Lady Honora said, her lips curling.

Helena suspected that Lady Honora found her unworthy of the title, but she was inclined to agree. She would prefer that Beatrice address her by her given name.

"Do you live at Ravensgrave?" Helena asked, seating herself on the settee beside Beatrice.

Lady Honora sat in the nearby chair and poured herself a cup of tea.

"I do," Beatrice said. "Though I have been away these past few days. I returned only yesterday."

"Indeed," Lady Honora said.

A new tension filled the room. Clearly, the circumstances by which Lady Honora had become Beatrice's guardian were less than ideal.

"I do enjoy Ravensgrave," Beatrice continued. "It provides the perfect atmosphere to feed the imagination."

"I suppose," Helena said.

"Do you enjoy reading novels?" Beatrice asked. "I am writing a novel set in Ravensgrave, something in the vein of Miss Radcliffe's works."

"Oh!" Helena exclaimed. "How delightful!"

"That is not the word I would choose for it," Lady Honora said. "Do not set it in Ravensgrave."

"Of course not," Beatrice said. "I will be careful. I intend to call the estate *Darkwood*, and I will ensure that none of the characters are recognisable."

Lady Honora looked quite tired.

"I do not know if you follow the *ton*," Beatrice said, turning to Helena. "Lady Caroline Lamb has recently been quite disgraced due to the publication of her novel *Glenarvon*. She based it on events from her life, and unfortunately, many of the portraits were recognisable and rather unflattering."

"I had not heard of that," Helena said.

"It is not worth reading," Lady Honora said.

"It has its merits," Beatrice argued.

"Anyway," Lady Honora said. "There is much that you need to learn about being the Duchess of Ravensgrave. I would like to discuss some of those things."

Beatrice frowned, looking a little vexed.

"I have heard that you were working in the garden," Lady Honora said.

"It seems you are well-informed," Helena said dryly. "You need not worry, my lady. I have an entirely scientific interest in botany. I have no intention of letting anyone see me garden when we are in London during the Season."

"The *ton* would certainly talk," Beatrice said lightly. "A duchess with dirt on her hands—imagine the horror. But that would not be the worst scandal our family has endured."

"Be that as it may," Lady Honora said. "We will already be the topic of discussion, and I would prefer that Helena not draw more attention than strictly necessary."

"Of course," Helena said tightly.

Lady Honora took a sip of tea. "I know that you must miss your former life."

"I do," Helena said, unthinkingly. "Silence most of all."

Lady Honora's face hardened. "You have the biting wit of a lady. I suppose that is better than nothing."

"Yes," Beatrice said, sounding amused.

Helena poured herself a cup of tea, recognising the familiar scent of mint. "I am curious," she said. "Does Lucien always drink valerian root tea?"

Beatrice nodded. "He has terrible headaches."

"I suspected as much."

Valerian root was also said to be of use in melancholy, although Helena was not entirely convinced that the claim was supported by research.

"You are so knowledgeable," Beatrice said admiringly. "In the novel I am writing, there is a poisoner. Would you read what I have written and tell me if the portrayal seems accurate?"

Lady Honora gasped with such force that Helena nearly laughed. "How horrid! Why would you choose to write something so absurd? And to set it in Ravensgrave, no less!"

"Because Ravensgrave looks like the place where you would poison someone!" Beatrice exclaimed, laughing. "The plot should always match the setting."

"Not always," Helena said. "*Northanger Abbey* proves that. But I would be delighted to read your novel. I am quite starved for suitable fiction."

"Oh!" Beatrice cried, leaping to her feet. "You must come see the library!"

"The library is my nephew's study," Lady Honora said.

"Only because his study was burned to ash," Beatrice returned, waving a dismissive hand. "I am certain my cousin will have no qualms with his wife looking at our impressive collection of books."

Lady Honora sighed. "We need to discuss Helena's new duties."

Helena had just been offered a plausible escape, and she was going to take it. "I am certain that a visit to the library—or study, whichever the case may be—will not take very long," she said. "I will discuss them with you later. Perhaps, Lucien—"

"His Grace," Lady Honora said sharply.

"—will be inclined to join us," Helena finished.

"Wonderful!" Beatrice linked her arm with Helena's. "Let us go!"

They quickly left the room, Beatrice leading the way.

"Thank you," Helena said.

Beatrice laughed. "I know my aunt can be a little intense," she whispered conspiratorially. "You must try not to be too wounded by her. I believe she is a little threatened by you."

"Threatened?"

Beatrice nodded. "My aunt has suffered much in life. She has been forced to be strong and to make unfathomable sacrifices, and as a lady, I think she has often felt unappreciated for them."

"I see."

"It is difficult for her, having another woman about," Beatrice said, voice softening. "Especially one who is of a higher rank, as you are."

Helena bit the inside of her cheek. Although she suspected that she and Lady Honora would never like one another, she understood why she might feel a little uncomfortable in those circumstances.

"Here we are," Beatrice said, pulling open the intricately carved door.

As Helena entered, a prick of longing bloomed in her chest. The library was massive. Leather-bound volumes filled the giant rosewood shelves. Beatrice stepped lightly across the floor and drew back the draperies, illuminating the room. It reminded Helena of her father's glorious library, most of it sold and gutted to cover the family's debts.

The furniture was red and gold, and the room carried the faint scent of fire. As she entered, she spied an empty hearth. Beatrice had paused by a desk and chair. She lifted a book and tilted her head, reading the spine. "My cousin appears to be frustrated this morning."

"Why do you say that?" Helena asked.

Beatrice offered the volume. "He always reads Marcus Aurelius when something is distressing him."

Perhaps it is his new wife!

Amused at her own observation, Helena opened the book. Neat rows of printed Latin were complemented by scrawled translations and notes. Some pages contained tiny, hastily drawn pictures. Helena could find no rationale for those, for the images bore no clear relation to the content of the Latin. Perhaps Lucien merely drew when he was bored.

The table held pen and ink. Inspiration struck. Helena turned to a page with sufficient space and carefully drew a delicate thread of ivy leaves spilling down from the corner of the page.

"You are very talented," Beatrice observed.

The door opened behind them, and Helena looked over her shoulder. Lucien had entered.

"Why are you in my study?" he asked.

"I was told it was a library," Helena answered, turning back to her ivy. "I am trying to concentrate."

For a heartbeat, no one spoke. Then Lucien sighed. "Beatrice, I wish to speak privately with my wife."

"Of course," Beatrice said. "I will leave my manuscript for you later, Helena."

"I look forward to reading it."

As Beatrice left, Helena kept drawing her ivy. What did her husband wish to discuss? A shiver traced the path of her spine. She could not have said whether her reaction stemmed from fear or uncertainty. She still did not know this man.

"What are you drawing in my book?" His breath was hot against her ear.

Helena startled, having not heard his approach. He stood behind her and placed one hand on either side of her, effectively pinning her against the desk. Her breath shuddered in her chest. She grasped the pen so tightly that her hand ached. She felt his heat at her back, and a strange tension curled inside her chest. Her pulse jumped.

No man had ever stood so near to her.

"Did it occur to you that I might not want you drawing in my books?" he asked, low.

It had not.

"Am I distressing you?"

She paused, dipped the pen, and pressed the nib beneath her trail of ivy, watching the bead of ink form there.

"Very much. You have distressed me since the day we met."

"I feel similarly about you."

Most roots thrive in shadow, Helena wrote in her fine, looping hand.

"Give me the pen."

She did, anticipating that he would move away, but he did not. Instead, Lucien pressed his chest more firmly to her back—possessive, contained. Heat rose to her face. This was probably not proper behaviour.

Helena swallowed hard. The pen scratched against the paper, and she watched as Lucien wrote, *Do you expect to win me over with empty platitudes?*

She inhaled sharply.

Lucien placed the pen on the desk. Helena seized it.

He laughed, the sound reverberating through his chest. It was impossible, but Helena swore she felt the show of amusement.

She wrote, *Who says that I am trying to win you over? I have already achieved my goal.*

Lucien moved away and dropped into the chair. He crooked a finger, beckoning for the pen. Helena surrendered it.

Unfortunate, he wrote. *You have no other ambitions in life.*

Helena frowned, a little affronted. She snatched the pen with more force than necessary. Lucien smirked.

As Helena pressed the nib to the paper, the absurdity of the exchange swept over her. She laughed.

I do have other ambitions. Maybe someday I shall share them with you.

Chapter Seven

Strange things were happening at Ravensgrave, and all of them had begun when Helena arrived.

Chief among them was her lady's maid, Meg—a woman who seemed to vanish without warning and reappear only in the kitchens to beg for food.

Items went missing, though not the usual sort that might suggest a thief. They were smaller things, easily overlooked: linens, books, sticks of charcoal.

Once a child's primer vanished from the schoolroom; another morning a basket of apples was found with two gone and the remainder neatly covered.

The housekeeper muttered about careless maids, the footmen denied all knowledge, and the matter drifted into that uneasy category of things best not examined too closely.

The second oddity was Helena herself, whom Lucien had glimpsed wandering the corridors late at night. Something was amiss.

For weeks, he had debated whether such peculiarities warranted confrontation. She was not malicious—merely strange—and perhaps that was to be expected of a naturalist's daughter with a fallen name.

Besides, there were greater concerns pressing upon him. The steward required decisions, tenants required coal, and the north roof leaked whenever the wind turned east.

The carriage jolted to an abrupt halt. Across from Lucien, Helena pitched forward, nearly tumbling into him.

"The *ton* will be watching us closely," Lady Honora declared sharply. "We must be strategic this evening."

"You make the whole assembly sound rather tedious," Beatrice said, her bright eyes darting to the carriage door.

"You take the least charitable understanding of everyone's words," Lady Honora snapped. "The assembly will be perfectly adequate. However, it is Helena's introduction to society. After the mess last Season, we can afford no further scandal."

Beatrice looked suitably chastened.

The footman opened the door, and they descended from the carriage. Lucien offered his arm to Helena, who hesitated only briefly before placing her gloved hand on his sleeve. She looked every inch a duchess.

The Marchioness of Pellam's invitation had arrived too late for Helena to visit the modiste, so she had borrowed a gown from Beatrice—a black velvet creation, hastily embroidered with ivy at the waist and hem.

It suited her surprisingly well, the dark material lending her auburn hair a luminous glow. Her figure was elegant, her posture composed. A narrow bracelet of jet lay cold upon her wrist; the only colour was the faintest blush at her throat.

"Shall we?" Lucien asked.

"Yes."

"Try not to hurl mud at anyone," he murmured under his breath.

Lucien was only half in jest; he could easily imagine his wife resorting to such behaviour if provoked.

"Try not to be so infuriating," she returned evenly.

He smirked. "Do you know what occurs to me? It makes no sense that you accosted me at all. Why didn't you speak to my driver?"

"I am hardly going to harangue some poorly paid employee of yours," she replied. "If the driver failed in his duties, the fault lies with his master."

Lucien laughed. "You possess an uncanny talent for turning every fault into mine."

"You make it too easy."

As they neared the entrance of Pellam Hall, Lucien's gaze fell upon the Marchioness herself—a tall, austere woman with silver hair and eyes as pale as winter skies. Her gown of black satin rendered her nearly colourless.

Lucien had always found her as warm as a granite column, but she was important and well respected. His aunt had nearly gone into raptures when the invitation arrived.

"The marchioness," he murmured to Helena. "She and my aunt share a temperament. If you can manage Lady Honora, you can manage her."

"Noted."

When they reached the Marchioness of Pellam, Helena curtsied gracefully.

"Your Grace," the marchioness said coolly. "I am so pleased you were able to join us this evening. It has been some time since you attended any formal engagement."

Lucien caught the implied censure. "Indeed. It is good to be among the *ton* again. May I present my duchess, Helena? My lady, this is Elaine, the Marchioness of Pellam."

"I am delighted to make your acquaintance," Helena said smoothly. "My husband speaks so highly of you."

"Does he?" The marchioness arched a brow. "I find that difficult to believe."

Helena's smile faltered; Lucien inwardly winced.

"You are Mr. Darrow's daughter, are you not?" the marchioness asked. "A peculiar choice for a duchess."

"Yes," Lady Honora said, gliding forward. "Lady Pellam, you are looking so very well."

Lucien had never been so grateful for his aunt in his life. He seized the opportunity to lead Helena away.

"She is *exactly* like your aunt," Helena murmured once they were out of earshot.

"Indeed. And I would not attempt to charm her again. She has no tolerance for empty flattery."

"I gathered as much."

As they entered the ballroom, Helena drew a sharp breath. "It is exquisite."

She was right. Ivy and holly twined about the white columns, while roses—red and white—overflowed from jewelled arrangements that glittered beneath chandeliers.

The vast marble dome arched high above, painted midnight blue and spangled with gold stars.

Musicians in livery sat beneath a gilded gallery; the soft bustle of silk and the faint clink of crystal made a kind of music of their own.

"Yes," Lucien said, watching her instead of the room.

She looked radiant, her eyes alight with wonder. That expression softened her face and rendered her quite breathtaking. A thousand eyes seemed to turn when she moved; even the murmur of gossip thinned, curious to see what sort of duchess he had married.

"Shall we dance?" he asked.

A lively waltz began, the violins quick and sweet. Helena nodded, and they stepped to the centre of the floor. Lucien could feel the gazes of the *ton* following them; whispers fluttered like moths around their names.

He drew her close, and she caught her breath.

"A warning would have been nice," she murmured.

Lucien's lips curved. "Have you ever seen a couple waltz at a distance?"

"We could be the first."

His hand found her waist, and she stiffened slightly before yielding. They moved together in time, her steps light, her frame graceful. Relief stirred in him—he had not known whether she could dance. Her glove brushed his knuckles; heat moved through him as cleanly as a blade through cloth.

As they turned beneath the lights, Lucien became acutely aware of her—the warmth of her body, the faint scent of lilac clinging to her hair. Desire curled low within him, slow and unfamiliar.

He had not felt such a thing in years. Duty, grief, and the weight of his inheritance had dulled all softer impulses. But Helena... she stirred something dangerously alive.

Her breath quickened; colour rose to her cheeks. He wondered if it was merely the exertion—or if she felt it too. The final figure drew them closer still; her lashes lifted, and the look she gave him landed like a touch.

The music ended. For a suspended heartbeat, neither of them moved. Lucien bowed, reluctant to release her. "Thank you for the dance. Enjoy the rest of your evening. I believe I shall take some air."

His pulse raced as he strode from the ballroom. Would the *ton* whisper that he had abandoned his wife after a single dance? Likely. He did not care. He needed distance—from her, from this suffocating stir of feeling.

The orangery loomed beyond the terrace, half-forgotten and overgrown. Its door stood ajar. Perfect.

Lucien slipped inside. The air was thick with the scent of damp earth and crushed petals, the glass panes misted by winter breath. It reminded him of Ravensgrave's ruined conservatory. A cracked marble nymph regarded him with blind serenity; a pot of orange trees had long since gone to leaf and thorn.

He braced a hand against the wall and exhaled. She had looked so lovely, so untouchably alive beneath the light. He could still feel the shape of her waist beneath his palm.

"Your Grace."

She stood framed in moonlight, that faint, defiant smile playing at her lips. "We looked convincingly in love, do you not think?"

"You overstep," he said, voice low but cutting. "I do not enjoy being made a spectacle."

"Then perhaps you should not make such an easy target."

His gaze hardened. "Careful." The single word landed like a warning.

"Am I to fear you, my lord?"

"You would be wise to respect me." He took a slow step forward, his shadow swallowing hers. "I could make you believe it—every look, every touch. I could make you love me if I chose."

"Bold words, Your Grace." Her tone wavered between challenge and surrender. "Are you so certain?"

He could have laughed it off, claimed jest, retreated into arrogance and scorn. It would have been safer. But safety was not what he wanted.

He stepped away from the wall and closed the distance between them. "I am never uncertain."

Helena did not retreat.

Lucien's mouth found hers, slow at first, then hungry. She gasped and lifted her arms, twining them about his neck. His hand gripped her waist, dragging her closer until there was no space left between them.

The kiss deepened, fierce and consuming. She tasted of wine and defiance. Her fingers tangled in his hair, pulling him nearer still. Outside, somewhere in the gardens, a fountain played—thin silver music that made their breathing sound louder in the glassy hush.

He kissed her as if it might burn the world away.

At last, she broke the contact with a ragged breath. They stood, chests heaving, the air between them charged and trembling.

A laugh—bright and feminine—split the silence. Ice shot through Lucien's veins. They froze.

"Helena?" It was Beatrice.

Lucien exhaled, half in relief, half in regret.

At last, he lifted his head, breathing hard, his thumb grazing her swollen lower lip. "That," he said quietly, "is how conviction feels."

A breathless pause. Then she whispered, "You take what you want, my lord."

Reality crashed back like cold water. Fool. What had possessed him?

"This cannot happen again," he said.

"Of course not."

Her composure stung him more than anger would have. She adjusted the neckline of her gown where his hands had strayed, and he looked away, ashamed by the heat still coursing through him.

"Helena?" Beatrice called again, further off this time.

"I will leave first," Helena said.

"Very well."

He opened the door for her. She passed him without a word, her perfume lingering like a memory he could not quite shake.

Lucien watched until she vanished into the shadows. His chest ached. A part of him wanted to follow, to taste her again.

He could not. He must not.

It had been nothing more than impulse—a curiosity, a moment's folly. It meant nothing.

It *must* mean nothing.

Chapter Eight

Helena woke before dawn. The kiss had been a mistake, a lapse in judgment.

It could not happen again.

She did not want it to happen again.

Despite her resolve never to kiss her husband again, her fingers drifted to her mouth. She imagined that her lips still tingled with the memory of her secret encounter with Lucien.

The room lay dim and grey; a strip of winter light crept along the floorboards, and the windowpanes wore a film of cold that blurred the park into a smear of ash and frost.

As the morning grew, she remained in her bedchamber. Meg always came to prepare her, but the woman had not yet arrived. Perhaps Edmund had kept her.

The house stirred: a scuttle of footsteps along the corridor, a coal-scuttle rasping, the muffled thud of wood upon the kitchen range carried faintly up the flue.

An hour past Meg's usual time, Helena began to worry. Something was wrong. She hurriedly dressed in a quiet gown. She considered her hair and left it loose.

A respectable lady would have pinned it up, but a pressure had risen in her chest; she suspected that something had gone terribly wrong. She paused only to draw a shawl about her shoulders—the wool smelt faintly of lavender from last summer's chest—and listened, as if the house itself might tell her what awaited.

There was a knock at her door. "Enter!"

One of the maids peered in. "I beg your pardon, Your Grace, but His Grace wishes to speak with you in his study."

"Can he wait?"

The maid blinked, startled. "I do not believe so, Your Grace. He spoke as if it were an urgent matter."

Helena froze. What if Meg had not come because she had been found out? She drew a deep breath and forced down the lump that rose in her throat. "Very well."

She slipped on her slippers and set a brisk pace through Ravensgrave. Her heart hammered as she tore open the library door. The portraits in the passage—solemn men in black and women in pearls—seemed to watch her pass with fixed, cold interest; the long runner dulled the sound of her steps, but not the beat of her pulse.

Her worst fears were confirmed. She halted on the threshold like a frightened creature caught in a snare. Meg and Edmund were seated, both pale and awkward. Lucien paced behind his desk, his expression unreadable. "How good of you to join us."

His voice was not cruel. It was eerily calm.

The calm before a storm, Helena thought.

"You might have warned me," Lucien continued. "About the extra portions of food. About your maid stealing from me. About the child I did not know I was sheltering."

Helena's throat went dry. She wet her lips, seeking words that would not come.

"Well? Have you anything to say for yourself, my dear and deceitful wife?"

She met his gaze unflinchingly and crossed to them, halting beside Meg and Edmund. "You married me for convenience," she said. "You did not marry me for my honesty."

"Oh?" He laughed once. "Is that your grand rebuttal? I rather think a certain level of honesty is implied in marriage."

"You are mistaken."

"Am I?" Lucien clenched his hand atop the desk. The crack in his composure showed. "You smuggled a child into my house. This is not some little deceit."

"That child is my brother Edmund. He is not a spy or a threat or even a stranger," Helena snapped.

"And why exactly did you see fit to hide him?" Lucien asked. "Are you mad? What possible justification had you?"

Edmund shifted uneasily and bit his lip. He looked anxiously between them. Helena gave him a reassuring smile and curled her fingers over the back of his chair.

Her mind raced, searching for some gentler answer than the truth, for she suspected Lucien would not relish knowing she had been afraid of him.

"There are already so many ghosts at Ravensgrave," she said at last. "It seemed unlikely you would notice one more."

"That is not an answer."

"It is an answer. You would only prefer a different one," Helena returned. "You have your secrets. I believe I am entitled to a few of my own."

"You are not."

"Your Grace—" Meg began, but Helena quieted her with a look.

"You will speak to me, rather than to them," Helena said, her voice trembling slightly.

"You presume to instruct me whom I may address," Lucien replied. "Have you forgotten, my lady-wife, that I am master of Ravensgrave? You do not dictate to me."

Helena bristled. Her instinct was to argue, and yet he was correct in all the ways that mattered. She was handling this poorly. If Edmund was to remain with her, she must salvage something.

"I misspoke, Your Grace."

The words were proper and contrite. They did not sound like her, but perhaps he would value them. If not, perhaps they would at least appease him.

Something shifted, and Helena could not tell whether for better or worse. Silence thickened between them like the fog that wrapped Ravensgrave before dawn. She dug her nails into the carved chair, enduring it. She had always hated such silences, but any words might anger him further. The clock upon the mantel ticked with small, irritating precision; a coal settled in the grate with a fall of ash.

"Do you comprehend the absurdity of this?" Lucien asked at last. "You expect me to overlook thefts within my household and an entire hidden child, and you offer no satisfactory explanation."

"I do."

He shook his head, and her heart sank. "You are... impossible. Quite as mad as I thought you the day I met you."

"I had a perfectly rational explanation for—"

His look silenced her. "By all means," he said, sweeping out a hand. "Enlighten me, my lady. I await it most eagerly."

"It is not one you will like," Helena said, temper fraying. "It will only provoke you further."

"You are not making a particularly strong case for why I should play reluctant guardian to a small boy. I would be justified in casting you all out."

Edmund gasped. "No!"

"No?" Lucien said.

"I told you that you would speak to me," Helena said quickly.

"And I explained that your wishes do not govern mine." He fixed his gaze upon Edmund. "What have you to say to me?"

"I do not want you to make us leave," Edmund whispered. "Or to make my sister leave. You should not be angry with her. She is very good."

"Doubtless you possess worldly experience enough to judge it," Lucien drawled.

"Now you will be cruel to a child?" Helena flared, fury rising.

"You are determined to make me the villain," Lucien cut back. "All the wrongdoing is yours, yet you contrive to blame me."

"Only because you are being entirely tedious," she said. "It does you no harm if my brother stays with me."

"Then why did you not tell me?" he demanded. "You are the most unpleasant and needlessly complicated woman I have ever met. Do you delight in tormenting me?"

"I might ask you the same."

Silence again. Lucien crossed his arms and leaned a shoulder against the bookshelves. Helena held his gaze and tried to ignore the panic beating in her blood. The scent of ink and old leather rose from the desk; Edmund's small hand crept towards hers along the chair-back, and she caught it with a swift squeeze.

Belatedly, she saw how poorly she had pleaded her case. Contrition had lasted only moments; her temper had done the rest.

"I have some conditions," Lucien said at last.

Helena let out a breath. "I will hear them."

"How gracious of you."

She smiled tightly.

"Meg will remain—officially—in your household. There will be no further pilfering of any kind."

"That will be no difficulty," Helena said.

Meg nodded.

"Ravensgrave is no place for a child," Lucien went on, "and I will not have a boy roaming at will and making mischief."

"Edmund will not," Helena said.

"No, Your Grace," Edmund added, eyes very wide. "I promise."

"Beatrice has taken it upon herself to index the books," Lucien said. "Here and elsewhere. Before the fire, we had two libraries; one was burned, and some volumes survived. Your brother may assist her." He spoke without softness; even his concessions were measured like an account.

That was not as dreadful as Helena had feared. Beatrice was cheerful and kind; she would doubtless dote on Edmund. The work would give him occupation and safety.

"Your terms are reasonable. Thank you."

"Do not thank me," he said curtly. "These are not kindnesses. They are conditions."

Helena inclined her head. He had not forgiven the deception, far from it, but he would leave matters as they stood for the present. It was more than she had expected.

"I understand perfectly."

"Good. And tread softly, my wife. I do not trust you. I will be watching to ensure you have not secreted any further children within the walls."

"Of course not. Only the one."

Lucien lifted a dismissive hand. "You may go. Keep the boy with you until the housekeeper finds a proper place for him. He will not return to that ruined nursery."

"Very well."

Helena rose and curtsied to show she truly understood. His frown deepened. She had disappointed him, and she suspected it would take considerable work to repair that damage. That was a problem for another time.

She took Edmund's hand, and they left the study. Meg followed. In the corridor, out of range of Lucien's gaze, Helena sagged against the wall. The hush of the passage swallowed them; cold breathed along the stone.

"That was terrifying," she said.

"I know," Meg murmured, twisting her hands in her skirts. "Oh, Helena—I am so sorry. I swear we were quiet. I do not know how His Grace came to find us."

"He found you himself?" Helena asked. "I can think of no reason he would go to that wing."

"Perhaps inspecting the damage," Meg said. "Or perhaps someone spoke—only a word, and not meaning harm."

"Did we cause you trouble?" Edmund asked.

Helena shook her head. "Not at all. Lucien was merely surprised; and in truth, I ought to have told him about you long ago. It has been weeks."

When she considered it, even she was not entirely certain what had governed her delay. At first, she had intended to wait until she had learnt more of Lucien's character; then weeks slid by, and still she had not. Perhaps some part of her did not wish him ever to meet her brother—did not wish to mark, by that introduction, how irrevocable her choice had been. Her palm still remembered the weight of the ring; the gold felt heavier this morning than it had yesterday.

"It might have gone worse," Meg said.

"Indeed," Helena agreed. "Edmund, I will show you to my bedchamber. Meg, will you find breakfast for us all? I think it best I remain in my room for the rest of the day. Lucien will hardly care to see me again, and he may wish to speak with Lady Honora before I do."

She winced inwardly, imagining how he might recount the matter; yet she doubted even he could make it sound worse than it was. The house creaked softly as if in assent.

"I will," Meg said.

Helena smiled and winked at Edmund. "Let me show you my room. It is much larger than the one I had in London."

Edmund grinned. "Because you are a duchess now."

"Yes, because I am a duchess."

Even if she did not feel like one.

Chapter Nine

Lucien spent most of the day in his study. His efforts at industry were all for naught; his thoughts insisted upon Helena. The occurrence was becoming far more frequent than he liked. Their encounter that morning had been odd.

He had expected guilt and excuses. Instead, Helena had been unrepentant, comporting herself as though Ravensgrave belonged to her and she might do with it whatever she pleased.

His aunt had warned him about women who refused the background; he had answered with a sly remark. The woman had been entirely correct. He had brought this one upon himself.

A light knock sounded. "Come in," he called.

It was unlikely to be his wife. She never knocked. The door creaked; Peter Langford stepped in. "Good evening, Your Grace."

"Good evening."

Langford would be there to review the estate, as he did weekly. A spark of guilt pricked Lucien for having let the hour slip; the clock on the mantel had advanced almost a full quarter beyond the appointed time. Outside, wind pressed at the casement; a thread of cold bled in at the joinery.

"Please sit," Lucien said. "I was reviewing the ledger just before you arrived."

A lie, betrayed by the hasty shuffle of papers. Langford lowered himself into the chair opposite without comment; if he noticed anything amiss, he was too well-bred to say so. The steward set a neat stack of memoranda upon the desk, each page pricked with tidy annotations.

"I have been noting the damage in the east wing," Lucien said, making his voice practical. "As much as I should like the manor restored, the wing must lie in ruins for now. Our time will be better spent elsewhere."

"Agreed," Langford said. "Your late father's investments do appear promising; funds should begin to flow soon. I have identified certain districts in the dukedom that would benefit from repairs—Moor End cottages, the mill roof at Harrow Beck, and the by-road from Stonegate to the north farms. The tenants petition for gravel and drainage."

Lucien glanced down the list; the familiar names settled him. Money, roofs, roads—these were matters a man could grasp with both hands.

It was unfortunate that his bride had brought no substantial dowry. A proper bride might have done so. Sometimes he wanted a proper lady—someone less contrary. It began to feel as if Helena took pleasure in making his days as difficult as possible; and yet, against his will, he had developed a liking for her. That, too, was inconvenient.

"Your Grace, shall we meet another time?" Langford asked gently.

"Pardon?"

"You seem—if I may—preoccupied."

"Do I?"

"Yes. You look a defeated man, in truth. Has something happened?"

"Helena has happened," he said drily. "She has altered certain expectations."

"With respect, Your Grace," Langford replied, "that is true of all marriages."

"Is it? I had anticipated—" He faltered.

"Anticipated what?"

"Something else. That she would tend to her own affairs and not meddle with mine. That she would join me only for society. Instead, she is making changes to Ravensgrave."

"Like a wife?" Langford asked mildly. "Keeping the house. Ordering it."

Given that Helena's "ordering" had included smuggling a child into the east wing, Lucien doubted she meant merely to arrange flowers and cushions. He had not yet settled upon what tale he should tell of Edmund Darrow—Darrow he remained, for now—so he only inclined his head, as though he agreed.

"You could do worse," Langford added.

"Certainly. But enough of Helena," Lucien said. "You came to discuss the estate."

"If you can remain with me, Your Grace," Langford said, smiling. "There are tenant petitions for your review." He lifted the first. "Mrs. Ainsley seeks relief on arrears after her husband's illness; she offers labour in lieu. The parson supports her claim."

"Granted," Lucien said. "Half remitted; the remainder to be worked off by spring."

"Very good." The steward's pen scratched. "The miller proposes to share thc expense of roof repairs if we match it."

"Match it."

"Lastly—coal allotments. The winter proves harsher than last."

"Extend them a fortnight," Lucien said. "No child will freeze for want of Ravensgrave coal."

Yet as Langford read on, Lucien's mind wandered. He nodded when required, granting what the steward deemed reasonable. If Langford thought a petition worth consideration, it was sufficient. The evening passed to the low hum of the steward's voice—and to thoughts of Helena's fierce green eyes. At length, Langford departed, leaving order behind him like a well-swept floor.

Lucien rose, his glance straying to Marcus Aurelius's *Meditations*. Had he been needlessly hard upon Helena that morning? The case was unprecedented; nevertheless... He, too, had secrets, many never shared; perhaps it was unfair to demand of her what he had not yet given. He touched the cracked leather of the spine and thought better of opening it.

Philosophy would not quiet a house set at odds.

***

At dinner, he found his aunt and cousin already seated; his wife was missing. The candles burned steady; the silver had been laid with a precision that reflected the chandeliers in small, bright moons. He took the head of the table and beckoned to a newly hired footman whose name escaped him. "Inform Her Grace that dinner is served. Tell her that Edmund is welcome to join us."

"At once, Your Grace."

"Who is Edmund?" his aunt asked, pausing with her napkin.

"Helena's brother," Lucien said. "He will remain for a time and assist Beatrice with the cataloguing of the books."

Lady Honora raised an eyebrow. "I was not aware she possessed a brother."

Lucien only shrugged. The servants began to bring the first course. He shook his head. "We will wait upon my wife."

"Assuming she comes," his aunt said. "Some women—who are not well-bred—take liberties once their position is secure."

She did not know even half of what Helena had done. Still, the condescension made Lucien bristle. A duke might rebuke his aunt; a nephew seldom did. He checked the impulse and folded his napkin instead.

Meg entered, Edmund clinging to her skirts. The woman curtsied so clumsily she nearly lost her footing. "Her Grace is unwell and begs to be excused. She sends her sincere apologies."

"She was in admirable health this morning," Lucien said drily.

"The illness came on quite suddenly, Your Grace."

"Evidently." He gestured to the empty chair beside Beatrice. "Edmund, sit."

Lady Honora's nose wrinkled, as if at an odour, while Meg settled the boy and backed away with another wobbling curtsey.

"Well," said Beatrice, with forced brightness, "I am famished. I suppose we may have the first course, though Helena does not join us."

Carrot and fennel soup arrived, steaming gently in the chill of the room. They ate it in stony quiet. The second course followed—salmon in pastry, a squeeze of lemon bright upon the air—then a saddle of mutton with caper sauce; even the excellent cook could not season conversation into them.

"So, Edmund—you are very fortunate in your sister," Beatrice said, valiantly warming the air. "Few ladies read as she does."

"I know." The boy's gaze flicked to Lucien, wary as a field hare.

Excellent. He was inadequate to Helena and to a child who disliked him upon sight. He carved, too neatly, and set down the knife before he drove it through the table.

Silence fell again. By the final course—pear tart and syllabub—Lucien would have sworn angels were singing. When the meal ended, he rose too quickly and forced a smile. "I shall retire."

"May I have a word?" Beatrice asked, rising at once.

"Of course."

He doubted he desired it; yet there was no reason to refuse. They stepped from the dining hall into the long passage where portraits watched with blank, ancestral calm. Out of earshot, he turned a look upon her. "You mean to chide me. What is the matter?"

"If I must guess," she said, "you quarrelled with Helena; thus her absence."

"So I did," he sighed. "It is of no consequence."

"Then make it so by making amends. She is more alive than anyone in this house; she will be good for you."

"Will she?" he scoffed. "You are certain, and yet we scarcely know her."

"Give her a chance. That is all."

"I have given her a chance."

"Have you?" Beatrice's eyebrow rose. "Or have you given her your rules and expected gratitude?"

His jaw tightened. "My life is being dictated by three women," he said. "You, my aunt, and Helena."

"How poetic. We are the three Fates." She grinned. "If you wish to begin amends, try the conservatory. It is beginning to feel... awake."

She winked—conspirator to conspirator—and went off humming. The echo of her steps trailed into the hush.

Lucien raked a hand through his hair and set towards the conservatory. The night wind bit his face; his breath frosted white upon the air. Frost feathered the lawn; the sky had the hard glitter of iron.

Frost cracked underfoot as he entered. A wan flame flickered—a lantern set upon a stone plinth, its glass clouded with breath. As Beatrice had foretold, Helena was there. She knelt, trimming a dead strand of ivy. Despite the cold, her sleeves were rolled past the elbows; her skirts were hitched above the knee, showing the pale silk of stockings and the briefest crescent of skin. In the moonlight, she was too lovely for speech.

His gaze lingered on the revealed line of her back, the strict curve of her hip. Her shortgown lay discarded upon a bench; a pair of shears and a coil of twine kept it from blowing away in the draught. He swallowed. She put him in mind of a white stag in a winter wood.

"Do not look at me like that," she said.

He did not stop.

"What was it you said in the orangery?" he asked, smiling. "Ah—were you afraid we might look convincingly in love?"

"That is not precisely what I said."

He might have teased her about their first encounter; he found he did not wish to spoil the moment.

"I am taking liberties," he said, "as you are taking liberties with what a duchess ought to be."

"Your criticism is duly noted."

"I did not intend it for criticism."

She rose, wiped her palms on her skirt, and turned to face him. Her face was pale in the moonlight; her red hair had come slightly loose; a small streak of mud ran along her cheekbone. Her breath smoked lightly in the cold.

"Why did you not dine with us?" he asked. "You are plainly not struck down by sudden illness if you can trim ivy in a freezing conservatory."

"I had no appetite—either for food or for performance."

He gave a low laugh. "So, you prefer thorns to company."

"After being cornered in your study, I preferred dying plants to cold hosts."

He stepped nearer, the lantern striking a hard gleam across his cheek. "You mistake command for coldness. Do not do so again."

"Or what, Your Grace?" Her chin tipped, defiant.

"Or you will discover I am far less patient than I was this morning." His gaze dropped, unhurried, to the mud upon her cheek and the pale edge of her knee above her stocking. "You knew what you were about."

"Did I?" she asked, breath a shade too quick.

He let the beat draw tight between them, then spoke softly. "Look at me, Helena."

She did. For a moment, neither of them moved. The glass gave a faint tap as a drop of melt fell.

"Well?" she said, eyes bright.

"Nothing that concerns your safety," he answered, voice even. "For tonight, I shall not quarrel with you. But you will not slight my table again."

Doubt crossed her face, as if she hardly believed him. With every heartbeat, he expected she would rise and sweep past him into the night.

At last, her expression softened. "It will take time. The ivy has been fiercely neglected."

"I know."

"You ought to be ashamed," she added, arching an eyebrow, daring him. "To have treated the vines so shamefully."

"I agree," he said, and after a breath, "You will dine with me tomorrow."

Her smile came hesitant and edged. "Very well."

She turned away and crouched again, hitching her skirts a fraction higher. His eyes rested on the bare span above her stocking; a pleasant shiver went through him as she set the trowel and loosened the strangling growth. The scent of damp earth rose, clean as rain after smoke.

Her work in the conservatory no longer vexed him.

He liked her thus—in the moonlight, at labour, waking the place.

He supposed he ought to return her trowel.

Chapter Ten

Hours after waking, Helena remained in bed and stared at the ceiling above her. The canopy's fringe hung still as icicles; a faint crack ran like a vein through the plaster. She curled her fingers in the bed linens, trying to make sense of the events of the past couple of days.

It would be easy to hide again. If she remained in her room, she could be herself, rather than act the Duchess of Ravensgrave. The word *obey* from the vows seemed to linger in the air like winter breath.

But no—

She would not hide from anything. Not from Lady Honora's disdainful looks or snide remarks. Not from the glances of the staff, which she sensed more than saw. And most certainly not from Lucien, the most infuriating man in all Britain. She did not like the side of him that had shown itself these past days, least of all in the study, where every panel of wood seemed to listen.

His words still rang in her ears: "You presume to tell me whom I may speak to. Have you forgotten, my lady-wife, that I am the lord and master of Ravensgrave? You may not dictate to me."

She would concede she had not answered him perfectly, but the remark did not bode well. He meant to put her in her place, to force her to relinquish her freedom. The day might come; she would not bend easily.

Somehow, she must reassert herself. She must show Lucien that she would not be cowed. Decision made, she swept the bed linens aside. She would move through the manor as though nothing required explanation. Helena slipped into the parlour attached to her bedchamber. Meg and Edmund sat at a low table, playing chess. The black queen lay toppled; Edmund's white knight advanced like a small, defiant banner. Helena stifled a laugh, for Meg was losing badly.

That was on purpose, no doubt.

"How are my two favourite people this morning?" Helena asked.

Edmund did not smile, and her spirits dampened at once. "Is... is he going to make us leave?"

Helena shook her head. "No, dearest. You need not worry about Lucien." She kept her voice as cheerful as she could, hoping her brother would not hear the tightness in it. "You will index the library with Beatrice. She is very kind. And I will be the duchess here."

"But what if he separates us?"

All of Helena's old fears re-emerged, fingers of ice clawing at her heart. She was a duchess; Edmund was to be safe. Yet she wondered if she had traded one enemy for another, more dangerous one.

"No," Helena said, her voice unsteady. "Lucien is a little frightening, but he is not so cruel."

"That is right," Meg put in. "The two of you will be together always."

Helena nodded. "Right. Well. I am going to face the morning."

"We were thinking of visiting the gardens later," Edmund said.

Helena glanced through the window overlooking the grounds. The sky was blue and full of white, woolly clouds. Sunlight shone upon the sparkling, frost-bitten grass and the gilded frame of the broken conservatory. Smoke drifted thinly from a distant chimney, straight as a rod in the still air.

"It is a beautiful day to be in the gardens," Helena said. "Soon it will be spring, and I daresay Ravensgrave will be alive and green."

"Yes," Meg said, brightening. "When it is, Edmund and I shall join you. Perhaps we might begin a new herbarium. Your mother taught me to press leaves between her sermons and her stories."

Edmund nodded, looking a little easier.

"Would you like assistance with your dressing?" Meg asked.

Helena shook her head. "No; continue your game. I can tend to myself."

She returned to her bedchamber and dressed in silence, taking little heed of which gown best became a duchess. A stout wool walking-dress, a plain chemisette, half-boots with decent soles—sufficient for thorns and cold stone. She coiled her hair without art and tied a ribbon at the nape. She meant to spend the day in the gardens. She had made good progress in restoring the conservatory to its former order, and Lucien had not seemed displeased.

Besides, the quiet there would give her time to think.

When she was ready, Helena kissed Edmund's hair and wished him luck in his battle with Meg, who was clearly endeavouring to hand him a victory. She smiled warmly at Meg; then she stepped into the corridor, resolved to be herself. The runner whispered beneath her feet; a draught teased the wall sconces.

She had set a brisk pace for the conservatory when a cloud of pink muslin and bouncing black curls intercepted her.

"Helena!" Beatrice cried, linking their arms. "Just the person I hoped to see."

"Oh?"

"You are bound for the conservatory?"

Helena laughed, a little taken aback. "Am I so predictable?"

"Yes, but that is quite well." Beatrice's smile was so infectiously bright that Helena could not help but answer it. "I shall walk with you. I think you will take interest in my latest novel."

"That is right. You promised me pages."

Beatrice nodded vigorously. "I was dissatisfied; I have begun anew. It shall be about a botanist and her scandalous protector."

Helena laughed. "That sounds rather—"

"Like you were the inspiration?" Beatrice's eyes danced. "Of course you were. Fear not; no one will know it. I have named the heroine Amelia; her hair is as black as night, and her eyes are blue."

"Will that suffice?" Helena asked. "You do not wish to be the next Lady Caroline Lamb."

They descended the stairs together, their steps chiming faintly upon the treads.

"The scandalous protector is entirely my invention," Beatrice said. "No one will recognize you. His name is Peregrine, the Marquess of Beaumont. He is mysterious; he may have committed murder. He haunts orangeries."

Helena raised an eyebrow. "I do not think Lady Honora will be charmed."

"Who cares?" Beatrice laughed.

"Not you, I suppose."

"Precisely. I intend a happy ending, however," Beatrice said. "I have not yet determined how I shall reach it, but I shall. Perhaps an elopement. Or a duel. I am undecided which is handsomer upon the page."

"I believe you; I cannot wait to see how you contrive it."

Beatrice grinned, halting at the garden door. "Excellent. I will leave the first chapter at your threshold. Enjoy your gardening, Helena."

"Thank you."

Helena watched her go, uncertain how she ought to feel about being the model for a heroine. At least, the scandalous protector would bear no resemblance to Lucien. *Peregrine* sounded the sort of man who invited ruin with a smile.

She shook her head and entered the conservatory.

***

Helena soon lost count of the minutes as she rolled up her sleeves and set to work. Despite the cold, she grew warm pruning roses and trimming vines. Sweat beaded her brow; clumps of earth smudged her forearms. She had abandoned her gloves, choosing convenience over protection, and had already paid for it—twice pierced by thorns. A pane rattled when the wind pressed its palm to the glass; a pale shaft of light fell across the cracked tiles like a benediction. The place smelt of damp, iron, and leaf-mould, with a breath of citrus when she bruised a dying leaf.

Behind her, the door creaked. Her breath caught. She had chosen the conservatory to avoid Lucien.

"You are remarkably consistent," he drawled. "Glass and thorns suit you."

Of course it would be him. She had not heard his approach; she straightened—and found his chest at her back, close enough that she felt the heat of him even in the chill. Leather and valerian brushed her senses. Instinct pricked; she jabbed her elbow into his stomach and whirled.

"I was just finished," she said, meaning to pass.

Lucien stepped into her path. "Stand still." Their gazes locked. After a heartbeat, his eyes flicked to her mouth. A slow, possessing smile touched his lip; she shivered. It was like a stroke of lightning: nerves alight, senses sharpened.

"No. You are not." His voice was a growl. "You will answer me before you run."

The world snapped into clarity. A terrible, impulsive idea presented itself—one that might let her reclaim some semblance of control after the humiliations of the past days.

She seized his lapels, pulled him down, and kissed him hard. She meant to draw away at once, but his arms closed about her waist; he dragged her flush, and her chest went tight. How dare he? How dare he ruin her attempt at mastery?

Without breaking the kiss, she caught his cravat and tugged sharply. He made a sound against her mouth; she could not tell if it was pain—or something else—but—

His hand brushed her thigh. Even through her skirts, she felt the heat of his palm. Her pulse leapt. It could become more. A dull ache threatened low within. It could not happen.

She would not let it happen. He would not win this silent contest. Panic scattered her thoughts like a dropped wine-glass on stone; she bit his lower lip.

He drew a breath and jerked back, blood bright upon his mouth. "Why would you do that?" he snapped, low and dangerous.

Colour rose to his cheekbones; he swore under his breath. Helena wiped her mouth and grimaced at the smear across her hand. Guilt sparked—and she smothered it.

"You should thank me for reminding you where we stand," she retorted.

"By biting like a rabid dog?"

"You touched my thigh!"

"I laid a hand upon my wife; you had your mouth upon mine. Do not feign surprise."

Helena laughed harshly. "It was no such thing. This is a marriage of convenience—"

"I am aware." His voice rose; anger hardened his face. "I signed the contract as well as you."

"Then act as if it were one, rather than lurking at every corner like a lecher."

"No. You will not lay this at my door," he said, fierce and controlled. "Not after the lengths to which I have indulged you."

"Indulged me?" She gave a scornful laugh.

"Yes. You hurled mud at me, and I still agreed to marry you."

"An act of desperation. This marriage serves you as well as me."

"I have let you alter my conservatory; I have allowed your brother here and not pried into any of your many secrets,"

Lucien shot back. "And every scrap of kindness I show you is turned into a weapon. It is intolerable."

"I beg your pardon for being such a burden," she said through clenched teeth. "It must be truly difficult to pretend to be something you are not."

"I have never pretended to be anything I am not."

"You do," she said. "You pretend at decency, only to be cruel another day."

Helena shoved past him, her face hot as an inferno. Fury blinded her. She longed to break something and could not. She ran for her bedchamber, ignoring the startled looks of two maids she passed.

"Are you well, Your Grace?"

No, she was not well. She would never be well so long as she was bound to that wretched man.

At her door, she nearly stumbled over a neat stack of papers tied with blue ribbon—Beatrice's novel. Helena snatched them up and burst into the room. Meg sat mending; seeing Helena, she started up.

"What has happened?"

Helena struggled to find her voice. "Wh—where is Edmund?"

"He is with Beatrice."

Her heart eased a fraction. Edmund would be safe and happy with Beatrice.

"It is nothing," Helena said softly. "His Grace and I argued. That is all."

Meg's face softened. "Will you speak of it?"

Helena rubbed the back of her hand against her eyes. "No. Not yet. Perhaps later."

Meg set the mending aside. "I shall draw a bath for you. After you have bathed and rested, it will not seem so dreadful."

"Thank you," Helena said, blinking against the warm rush of tears. "That would be very kind."

She went through to her bed and fell upon it, heedless of dirt upon the linens. The hearth ticked; a coal dropped, sending up one bright spark. Her fingers smoothed the first page. Beatrice had written the title in looping letters: *Nightshade Hall.*

Helena laughed at the absurdly obvious title, and despite the distress of the quarrel, she soon softened, calmed, in the decadent prose of Beatrice's melodrama. A wicked baron, a hidden staircase, a kiss in an overgrown arcade—nonsense, and yet exactly the sort of nonsense that steadied the heart.

Helena read every word.

Chapter Eleven

Lucien had spent the morning attempting to read tenant petitions, but by noon, he had managed to cover only a handful. The winter light fell white across the desk, turning ink to blue and paper to bone; the clock on the mantel ticked with a maddening serenity, as if time itself had no stake in a duke's affairs.

He read three sentences, and pictured Helena mud-streaked from the garden—the smear upon her wrist where ink had dried to a faint thread; the bare hands at dinner, startling for their frankness amidst cut glass and silver; the stubborn lift of her chin.

Then—the kiss.

It struck him again with such force that he was near breathless. Heat stirred within his chest and settled there, a coal refusing ash.

A knock sounded. "Enter," Lucien said.

Richardson stepped into the study and bowed. "A letter for you, Your Grace."

Lucien arched an eyebrow. "Place it there. I will read it when I have finished these petitions."

Richardson laid the letter at the desk's edge. Though Lucien had no intention of reading it yet, his breath hitched at the familiar seal. He took it up to be certain.

It was Sir Bertram Mallory's seal.

How... unusual.

"Do you recall—" Lucien broke off.

Richardson paused in the doorway. "Your Grace?"

Lucien pressed his lips to a line, thinking. He had a vague recollection of Sir Bertram once paying addresses to Helena, whom she refused. Shortly thereafter, she had another suitor—and drove the man to his death. The scandal sheets had made a feast of it; he remembered headlines laid out with vulgar relish beside coffee trays at gentlemen's clubs he no longer visited.

"Do you recall Lord Greene's death? It has been some time."

Richardson inclined his head. "I do. I believe it was said Her Grace was involved."

"What evidence was there? I seem to remember a letter."

"I believe there was also a servant's testimony," Richardson said. "And talk of an assignation."

Lucien drummed his fingers on the desk. "It is curious that Sir Bertram writes now. We have not spoken in years. He did not write after Henry's death, nor when I returned from Spain. Now I am married and suddenly worth a letter."

Richardson frowned. "The timing is certainly odd, but I confess I cannot divine his purpose."

"Nor can I," Lucien conceded. "Perhaps he means to warn me."

"Perhaps. Shall I fetch Her Grace?"

Lucien smiled wryly. "Not at present. I will speak with her later."

The letter might be nothing. It was not worth alarming Helena if Sir Bertram penned only pleasantries written with a serpent's quill.

"That is all," he added, attempting to set his mind again to the petitions.

Richardson bowed. "As you wish, Your Grace."

Lucien rubbed the page's edge between forefinger and thumb, considering the letter anew. After a heartbeat, he cracked the wax and unfolded the paper, eyes lighting upon the familiar hand.

My dear Ashmore,

I hope all is well with you. I wish to extend an invitation for you to join the Greythorne Assembly on 12 February at Lakewood House. As I have the honour of hosting this year, I take particular pains to ensure a convening both efficient and agreeable.

If you are able to attend, it will be most convenient; certain matters touch upon your interest. It seems an appropriate time to review the land boundaries of your dukedom and to discuss the Duchess of Ravensgrave's current social placement, which has lately become a subject of remark among our acquaintance.

Lakewood House was Sir Bertram's seat. Lucien's eyebrow rose. Sir Bertram's influence seemed to have grown if he were to host the assembly. The phrasing—*touch upon your interest*—had the oily softness of a glove hiding a knuckle.

Lucien scowled and set the letter aside. *The Duchess of Ravensgrave's current social placement*—as though such a thing were matter for debate, to be weighed like grain upon a scale.

He shook his head. Whatever Sir Bertram's aim, this was no innocent invitation. Something was amiss, and he strongly suspected it touched his wife.

With a sigh of frustration, he abandoned the petitions and crossed the floor. He had no inclination to play some petty game with Helena's former, jilted suitor. He must speak with her before the assembly—hear her impressions of Sir Bertram, and what the man might want. In all likelihood, she would be in the conservatory or the gardens; both were looking markedly better for her efforts, their ruin disciplined into promise.

"Oh!" A startled cry cut through the air.

Lucien halted, his gaze snapping to the shelves beyond the study door. He rounded one and found Edmund seated upon the floor, his back to the bookcase, Henry's old fencing manual in his hands—pages foxed, margins annotated with Henry's quick, impatient hand. Lucien crossed his arms. "How long have you been there?"

Edmund scrambled up and bowed with such zeal he nearly toppled. "I—I was only arranging the books, Your Grace!"

"You have a singular method of sorting materials," Lucien said dryly.

Edmund coloured. "Apologies, Your Grace."

Lucien regarded the boy for a long moment. He had little experience with children, and he barely knew this one. The boy's boots were clean but scuffed, his hair ill-treated by an impatient comb; there was ink upon his cuff in a small crescent, as if he had fallen asleep over a page.

"My brother was an excellent fencer," Lucien said at last. "One of the best."

It had not availed him. Henry had died in a duel fought with pistols, not blades; steel could not shield a man from lead and pride.

"Truly?" Edmund's eyes shone.

"Yes." Lucien paused. "Would you like to play chess?"

"If you would like to play chess, I would oblige you," Edmund said shyly, as if uncertain how one addressed a duke without a handbook.

Lucien smiled wryly. "Come."

He led Edmund to the armchairs by the hearth, drew out the old chessboard, and set the men—box and rosewood, kings worn smooth where boyish thumbs had pressed them through wet afternoons. He thought of the other board—the one in the conservatory, a rook forever overturned.

He advanced a pawn. "I assume you know the game," he said. "Do you?"

"Helena taught me."

Edmund pushed his pawn to meet Lucien's.

"Is she a good player?" Lucien asked, shifting another piece.

"The best!" Edmund brightened. "She says the queen ought always to look dangerous even when she is merely biding her time."

Lucien was not certain a small boy—devoted to his sister— offered the soundest judgment, yet the maxim had a certain savage wisdom. He said nothing, sliding his men across the field.

"Do you like the estate?" he asked.

Edmund nodded, eyes wide. "It is like something from my mother's ghost stories!" he exclaimed. "Helena loves it, too. She says the stones remember."

"That is one way to style it," Lucien said. "Ghostly."

He remembered Helena's justification for hiding the boy. It seemed long ago, though only weeks had passed. She had said there were ghosts at Ravensgrave; perhaps she had been right. The house held laughter in the stairwells and silence in the corners; it held ash in its throat and music somewhere beneath the floors.

"Do you know why your sister wished to hide you?" Lucien asked.

"No." Edmund's brow puckered. "She only said I must be quiet."

Curious.

Edmund captured a bishop with clumsy triumph. The boy was no adept, but at his age, that was expected. "Nicely done," Lucien said. He answered with a knight, the L-shaped leap he had always favoured, and watched Edmund's mouth form a small *oh* of admiration.

They played on. The game ended with Lucien's victory, though he had made allowances; he would not dishearten his young opponent. Edmund looked at the board as if at a map he meant to master.

"Well," Lucien said, offering his hand, "that was an excellent game, good sir. We shall play again sometime."

Edmund shook with a grin. "You are almost as skilful as Helena!"

"Almost?" Lucien laughed.

"Almost," Edmund insisted. "No one can best Helena!"

Lucien put away board and men. "Then I must practise often if I am ever to best her," he said, amused. "Thank you for the warning; I shall not feel humiliated when she does. Now—shall we to dinner?"

Edmund nodded.

Lucien led the way. The morning's turmoil had softened over the board. The boy was quick and clever—and very like his sister when he fixed upon a thing.

In the dining room, Aunt Honora, Helena, and Beatrice were already seated. The candles set diamonds in the glass; the black stone of the walls drank the light and gave it back reluctantly. Lucien glanced over their faces, searching for any sign of fresh quarrel. He found none.

He took his place, and the meal began. Carrot soup came first, aromatic with fennel; then roasted pheasant beneath a gloss of its own juices; potatoes crisped and cut small; a dish of winter greens, obedient but not cheerful. Lucien ate in silence, content to let Beatrice fill the air with her cheerful opinions of Mr. Scott's *Lady of the Lake*. His aunt bore the discourse with strained grace; her sentiments on Sir Walter differed markedly, and she suffered rhyme as she suffered draughts.

"I do not wish to change the subject," Aunt Honora said at length. "However, I observed that Sir Bertram sent you a letter."

Helena started, as if struck. "Did he?" Her eyes flew to Lucien's face.

"He did."

"I can guess at his topic," Aunt Honora said. "It has been in the scandal sheets."

"The scandal sheets?" Colour drained from Helena's face, leaving her pale as any ghost. "What are they saying?"

Aunt Honora smiled sweetly. "Sir Bertram once had an interest in you—"

"This is well known," Lucien interposed. "It is no scandal."

Helena frowned, doubt tracing her delicate features. Lucien quelled a flare of vexation with his aunt. He had wished to speak privately with Helena; instead, the matter would be aired over soup and pheasant like any other dish.

He ought to have expected his aunt to know. Had she been at court, she would have been formidable.

"The scandal is that he desires her still," Aunt Honora went on. "He insists that—"

"It does not signify what he insists," Lucien said, turning a level look upon her. "Helena is my wife. Sir Bertram had his chance to win her favour and failed. That is the end of it."

"Agreed," Beatrice said. "Yet it is strange that he would…"

"Would what?" Helena asked softly.

"That the subject should be raised at all."

"Doubtless the subject is not Helena," Lucien said. "I suspect Sir Bertram has some other scheme, and she is merely a convenient means—either to distract from his aim or to discredit me."

"Why would he wish to discredit you?" Helena asked.

"Perhaps he would supplant Lucien," Aunt Honora said.

Lucien raised an eyebrow. "What do you know?"

"I know the Greythorne Assembly is soon, and that Sir Bertram has the honour of hosting."

Lucien smiled wryly. "I marvel at the speed with which you learn such things, Aunt."

"What is the Greythorne Assembly?" Helena asked.

"A gathering of powerful noblemen," Beatrice answered promptly. "They negotiate alliances and discuss estates."

"Policy, also," Lucien added. "The Duke of Ravensgrave has long held influence there. It is possible Sir Bertram means to enlarge his, since my family has... encountered difficulties of late."

Helena shifted, eyes upon her plate; colour rose in her cheeks. She seemed ashamed—as if the house's misfortunes were hers to mend.

"It matters not," Lucien said. "I have no patience for Sir Bertram's games, and he ought to be ashamed to drag you into them, Helena. You are a married woman. It is disgraceful to pine openly for another man's wife."

As he spoke, a fire curled in his chest. It was disgraceful—not merely that Sir Bertram should profess some sudden interest, but that he should use Helena like a piece upon a board. Lucien set his jaw; a fierce protectiveness rose in him with a swiftness that surprised him.

"You have my support," he added, "regardless of what Sir Bertram may say or do."

A new sobriety settled upon them, and silence followed. Across the table, his aunt's eyes narrowed in thought; Beatrice looked as if she would fling herself into the breach with a jest and thought better of it. Lucien chewed a roasted potato, mind working. Beneath the cloth, Helena's fingers touched the back of his hand—light, uncertain. He drew breath.

Memory of the kiss surged; his throat tightened. He turned his hand over, wholly attentive to the warmth and softness of her skin, and closed his fingers around hers. He did not let go.

He decided to ask her nothing.

He trusted her; if she wished him to know the truth of Sir Bertram and Lord Greene, she would tell him in her own time.

Until then, he would meet Sir Bertram at Lakewood, and if the gentleman wished to make sport of a duchess, he would find Ravensgrave's duke had teeth.

Chapter Twelve

In two weeks, they would attend the Greythorne Assembly. This was not the assembly, but it was a ball at Sir Bertram's estate. Lucien had told her apologetically of the invitation, watching her face as if anticipating refusal. She had wished to decline, yet knew at once it would be taken for a slight. If she were absent, her absence would be remarked upon; it might place Lucien in a worse position at the assembly, which she knew was important to him.

Helena dressed in silence. Within, she shook. She had not seen Sir Bertram Mallory since he contrived to ruin her. She had no proof of his machinations, but she knew instinctively he had been responsible for the letter—allegedly written in her own hand—in which she had urged Lord Greene to slay himself. She suspected him, too, of prompting the testimony of the young maid Amelia Mitchell, who swore Helena had toyed deliberately with Lord Greene's affections. And now she must go to Sir Bertram's house before all the eyes of the ton.

"The gown looks exquisite," Meg said, appearing in Helena's mirror. "You look just like a duchess."

Helena bit the inside of her cheek and tried to calm her racing heart. The gown was unquestionably lovely—the same blue-grey as a storm-lit sky. Silver thread, embroidered into wildflowers and thistle, trailed along hem and cuffs. It was more fashionable than her usual gowns, yet the floral patterns were hers.

"Lovely," Beatrice said, weaving a strand of ivy into Helena's chignon. "You look a noble heroine."

Did she? Helena bit her lip. She could not quite banish the sense she was a child playing in garments not her own. However beautiful she entered, even upon Lucien's arm, people would see what they wished: the disgraced naturalist's daughter who had jilted one respectable suitor and led another to his death.

"I am ready," she said.

"You will do wonderfully," Beatrice answered. "My cousin will protect you, and Sir Bertram will—he will not so much as approach. There is no reason to be afraid."

Helena forced a smile. "I know, and I am very grateful to him."

They left her bedchamber and descended. Lucien and Lady Honora were already waiting. Seeing her, Lucien came to meet her at the foot of the stair. His gaze ran over her, lingering at her waist and neckline; heat prickled along her skin beneath that regard.

He said nothing of the gown, only offered his arm as usual. "Thank you," she said softly. "I confess I am terribly anxious."

"I understand," Lucien said, cool and sure. "No sensible woman would meet such a night without caution. But you are under my protection. While I stand, he will not come within an arm's length of you."

As he led her across the foyer, she felt his gaze return to her, taking her in. A small thrill went through her at that attention. He had said nothing of her appearance, yet she felt he had noticed a difference—and approved.

He handed her into the carriage; she settled beside him. Lady Honora and Beatrice sat opposite. It was not a long journey; Helena could not decide if that were blessing or curse.

"It will doubtless prove memorable," Lady Honora said, folding her hands. "Helena, you must be very careful. We require you to be a proper duchess."

Helena swallowed and kept her indignation from her face. Lady Honora spoke as if Helena had no notion of conduct. She did not know everything a duchess must know, yet she was well-mannered enough. Her father had been a gentleman. It was not as though Lucien had plucked her from the gutter.

Admittedly, she had very nearly fallen into it, but that did not bear mention.

"I am certain Helena's behaviour will not be the problem," Lucien said, the words edged with iron. "If Sir Bertram means to make mischief, he will do so; and if he does, he answers to me."

Lady Honora's lips curled. "Perhaps you are right."

Helena turned to the window, the curtain not quite drawn. Through the gap, she spied the moors with sweeping grasses and small, hopeful blooms. She imagined slipping from the carriage, losing herself in that sea of green, contending only with wind and sunlight.

Perhaps Sir Bertram would be taken ill and not appear at all. It was an absurd hope, but she clung to it.

"Did you—" Beatrice broke off.

Helena looked to her.

"What is it?" Lady Honora asked sharply.

Beatrice looked guilty. "I had a question, but I think it may be too personal. Best not to ask."

Lady Honora sighed as if some monstrous inconvenience had been offered. "You might as well ask."

Beatrice bit her lip, her eyes flicking to Helena's face.

Ice crept through Helena, yet she smiled. "You may. I am certain you both have questions for me."

Lucien's gaze rested steadily upon her. He must have more questions than aunt and cousin together, yet he kept them. Gratitude warmed her. She did not love him; yet since Sir Bertram's letter, something in his manner had softened. She liked him more than she had. She felt she might trust him. If he said he would defend her, he would. He asked nothing—but she knew he wished to.

"I wondered whether you were ever attracted to Sir Bertram," Beatrice said delicately.

"You need not answer," Lucien said at once. "If it is too personal."

"No," Helena said, her voice a little unsteady. "I was not. He was persistent. He would not accept my refusal. That is all."

She tried for lightness. She did not wish to load the evening with needless tension. Yet she remembered too well that there were hours when Sir Bertram had frightened her—his intensity, his refusal to be turned aside. Worse, he was famed for his charms; to speak ill of him was to invite disbelief.

"Oh, I am so very sorry," Beatrice murmured.

Helena nodded. "As am I."

Lucien's fingers stirred, as if he would reach for her, but he did not. She met his eyes; he smiled—brief, decisive—and something within her eased. She had him, at least. He would stand by her, whatever the night brought.

As they entered the ballroom, Helena's fingers tightened upon Lucien's arm. Her pulse thundered. Beatrice might call her a heroine, but Helena felt far too mortal for such a mantle.

Heads turned; fans lifted; voices dropped. She knew too well she was the subject.

The twice-disgraced naturalist's daughter. First, her father's madness; then accusation over Lord Greene; and now a marriage to Lucien that some would call opportunism, others punishment.

"Shall we dance?" Lucien asked. "I am fond of a waltz."

"Yes."

He led her to the floor, where couples were already turning. Helena's gaze sought Sir Bertram and did not find him. As host, he must greet guests; it was a small miracle they had not met him at the door.

A miracle—or a contrivance of timing. She suspected the latter.

"Look at me," Lucien murmured as the music rose. "Not at him. You dance with me; you attend to me."

His hand settled low upon her waist; she drew a steady breath and moved through the first figures, acutely conscious of his touch and the way he guided her. Heat from his palm sent a delicate shiver through her. Her back found his hand; with each turn, he drew her nearer, his lead certain and inarguable.

Her breath quickened. She glimpsed Sir Bertram—tall and broad-shouldered, dark hair, cold eye—then lost him again as the room revolved. If only he might be so easily vanquished— three steps, a turn, and gone.

Lucien's gaze darkened. A subtle change passed over him; he looked at her as if the world had narrowed to a single point. Had he seen Sir Bertram, too?

His grip firmed; his steps grew more decisive. When the room turned again, Helena found Sir Bertram's gaze upon her. He smiled. Breath shuddered in her chest. It was the regard of a hunter. He murmured to the lady at his side and began a slow approach.

"Hold to me," Lucien said under his breath. "He will not trespass while I am here."

The music ended. For a heartbeat, they stood close. Heat rushed through her; words deserted her. It felt like cliff-edge— an ache to cast herself forward and let whatever might catch her.

"Helena, what a pleasant surprise." Sir Bertram's light voice broke the moment.

Her shoulders tensed. Lucien shifted at once, placing himself a fraction before her—polite, implacable.

"Her Grace," Lucien said coolly. "In case you were unaware, Helena is now the Duchess of Ravensgrave."

Sir Bertram bowed, his amused smile unaltered. "I had not forgotten. We are old acquaintances, and I am delighted to hear she has married so well."

"Yes," Lucien returned through his teeth. "Which is why I do not understand your wish to discuss her 'position'."

Sir Bertram laughed lightly and shook his head. "Why, I only wished to enquire after an old friend. There is no harm in that, surely? I recall Helena—pardon, Her Grace—was very fond of poetry. Do you still find time for it, or does the estate deny you such pleasures?"

"You will address any enquiry regarding the Duchess to me," Lucien said, voice low and even. "You will not trespass upon her peace with your solicitude."

Sir Bertram's ease did not waver, but Helena saw the spark in Lucien's eye—an anger she had not witnessed in him before.

Whispers threaded beneath the music of the next set. Warmth unfurled in her chest, startling and keen. Her body felt suddenly, bewilderingly awake.

"Lucien," she said.

He tore his gaze from Sir Bertram and fixed it upon her. "Yes?"

He had done as he promised—shielded her, and without hesitation. Gratitude and a fragile happiness rose within her. She, bride of convenience though she was, had not been thrown to wolves.

"Perhaps—another dance."

"We will dance," he said, with a slight, cutting inclination to Sir Bertram. He took Helena's hand and led her back among the turning couples.

Chapter Thirteen

As they danced, Helena drew nearer to him. The heat of his body bled into her own; it became difficult to tell where his warmth began and ended, and she heard her breath quicken with every step. His gaze remained fixed upon her face, even as colour rose along his cheekbones. She could not decide whether it sprang from the encounter with Sir Bertram or from the exertion of the dance. And yet—

It was apparent that Lucien's thoughts were elsewhere, for he stumbled a little. He did not tread upon her toes, but it was a near thing. His hand, pressed firmly at her back, seemed to wander; his thumb traced idle shapes along her spine.

"Is something the matter?" she asked.

A thrill of delight shot through her. Something in the sight of him—flustered, distracted—appealed to her, sent a fissure of anticipation through her frame. He stumbled again.

"Am I distracting you?" Helena asked.

Something hard pressed against her stomach. She blinked, at first confused by what that unfamiliar thing might be. She was not some sheltered young maiden; she knew something of how a man's body worked. Helena inhaled sharply, her eyes widening. She must be mistaken.

"You are terribly distracting," he said through clenched teeth. "Come."

He took her hand and set a brisk pace away from the dancers. She hurried beside him, her skirts flaring about her legs. "Where are we going?"

She deliberately did not look at his trousers. Lucien did not slacken even when they were well clear of the ballroom. Helena struggled to keep pace with his long stride. Her slippers struck the cold stone; her breath rose in little puffs. At last, they reached a musician's balcony above an old parlour. She opened her mouth to ask again where they were—and what they meant to do.

Lucien opened his jacket, and all her thoughts crashed to silence. Air left her lungs in a sudden burst, and she saw plainly what had drawn him from the dance. No one with eyes could miss the bold swell at his thighs. A proper lady would turn away at such a scandalous sight; Helena found herself frozen.

He set his fingers to his fall, seemingly oblivious to her astonishment. "Wh—what are you doing?" she stammered. "Why am I here?"

He fixed her with a stern, level look. "You did this. You have been pressed to me all night, and I could not very well parade it before the room."

Heat rushed to Helena's face; she covered her mouth with her hands.

"Besides," Lucien growled, "I would not leave you to that man. That rakish wretch. Now—make certain no one sees me while I tend to this."

A small, anxious sound escaped her as he undid the fastenings. His manhood sprang to his hand—hard and imposing. Admittedly, she had little frame of reference beyond a sculpture glimpsed in Italy and a physician's diagram, yet he seemed large. Her first shock faded, replaced by a nearly scientific curiosity.

"Unless you have a better idea?" he asked between his teeth.

She numbly shook her head.

"Then keep watch."

Helena turned, putting her back to him. A lump rose in her throat; her heart hammered. Behind her, Lucien gave a rough groan—the sound uneven, followed by ragged breaths. A dull ache curled low within her. She pressed her thighs together and set her fingers in her skirts.

Focus, Helena. You must see if anyone is coming.

But those sounds shattered thought. Every grunt, groan, and pant seemed to strike directly at her core. Her knees weakened with the realization that her husband was seeking relief not three paces behind her. She clenched her jaw. The ache grew more insistent with every sound he made; an involuntary whine tore from her own throat.

She could endure it no longer. Helena turned. Lucien's dark eyes met hers. His face was flushed, his lips a little parted, his expression startled. She wondered if her own face wore that same look of arousal. Her breath quickened; her breasts strained against the stays.

He held his hand firm about himself, the length reddened by his attentions. Helena took one step toward him. Then another.

He stilled. "What are you doing?" His voice was rough and low; it awakened the most wicked sensations within her.

"You are driving me to the brink of madness," she said.

Damp gathered between her thighs. Her body ached; a wild, improper thought rose of how he might find relief—through her.

"Am I?" He laughed without mirth.

She reached, tentative, and traced her thumb over the sensitive tip. He groaned; his body answered her touch at once.

"If I caused this, I should like to…" she faltered. "Perhaps I can…"

He tossed back his head and dragged in a breath. "Perhaps what?"

Steeling herself, she said, "Perhaps I can be of assistance."

After all, he had been good to her. He had defended her and kept Sir Bertram at bay.

She ventured another slow pass of her thumb; he hissed between his teeth. "Damn you."

Helena laughed, high and breathless. "That is unkind. I—I think this is…beneficial. I wish to leave before anyone discovers us—"

"You are going to be the death of me."

His left hand caught in her hair; he bent her to him and kissed her—hard, deep. She gasped; his teeth clicked against hers. Her thighs trembled; a fierce longing stirred. With his other hand, he guided her fingers. She wrapped her hand about him, eyes widening at the heat and weight.

"Knees," he said, a growl. "Now."

She sank. He loomed—broad, unyielding—and her pulse leapt.

"Oh, look at you," he murmured, both hands twined in her hair. "Hard, even strokes."

Helena watched her gloved hand moving along him and pressed more firmly. She stroked from root to tip and down again; his fingers tightened, and tears sprang to her eyes. It did not hurt—exactly—but each tug sent bright shocks to her core.

She fought the urge to hitch her skirts and ease the ache growing within. She worked her thumb across the crown, then along the length. He was so hot and iron-hard; she burned with want. If she let him, he might bury this within her. The thought shook her; her own inner walls clenched upon nothing.

"Both hands," he said.

She obeyed, one hand circling, the other teasing the tender place. His hips answered; his breath shortened to sharp, uneven pulls. The world narrowed to that single task—stroke upon stroke, steady as prayer.

His body shuddered with each touch; the motion set her slightly off-balance, and she adjusted, following the rhythm he set. She felt as though she climbed a ridge without a name, the air thinning, each step more perilous than the last. He gave a final, violent tremor and—

Lucien spent, thick and warm, spattering her gloves. Helena gasped. His grip loosened; she rocked forward a little, only then aware of the tension coiled in neck and shoulders. She pressed her knees together; the small pressure granted paltry relief.

"Oh—your gloves," Lucien said, raking a hand through his hair. "I did not think—"

Nor had she.

He drew out a handkerchief and offered it. "Do what you can."

Helena dabbed at the damp marks marring the kid leather. Suddenly, the fear of being found returned. She glanced about, then exhaled when the shadows yielded no one.

He tucked his shirt and set his buttons. After the briefest pause, he extended his hand. "You look very pretty thus," he said, eyes gleaming, "on your knees before me."

119

She hesitated before placing her hand in his. "I have ruined my gloves."

"Indeed."

He reclaimed the handkerchief and pocketed it, then smoothed his jacket. "I have quite ruined your hair."

She held still while he set her curls to rights. She willed her breath to slow, determined to appear composed. She ignored the pulse of need low within, the ache for his hand where no hand had yet touched.

"I suppose," Lucien said softly, "you will manage with your hands only this evening. We should not wish any person to remark on damp gloves."

Helena drew a sharp breath. "What a vulgar thing to say."

Yet the vulgarity made her toes curl.

He smiled and offered his arm. "Shall we return? We stepped out for air. That is why your cheeks are flushed. The night is brisk."

She laid her hand on his arm. They went back together in companionable silence. Helena felt something altered between them—an intimacy she would once have thought impossible.

"Thank you," she said softly. "For everything."

He gave a low laugh. "I believe conventional thanks belong to me."

"Then we shall thank each other."

They entered the ballroom. To Helena's immense relief, no heads turned; no eyes swept over them. Their absence, apparently, had gone quite unnoticed.

Lucien guided her toward the side where the tall windows let in a stripe of moonlight upon the marble. He fetched her a glass of lemonade from a passing footman; she kept her hands folded round her fan to hide what could not be explained. The orchestra had begun a country-dance; laughter rose and fell like surf against the shore. Lady Honora stood at a distance, deep in talk with the Marchioness, and did not glance their way. Beatrice, bright as a lark, waved and returned to her set.

"Keep near me for the remainder," Lucien murmured, pitched for her alone. "It discourages impertinence."

"I have no wish for impertinence," she returned, equally low.

"Good."

They moved a little further into the light. If any person marked them, it was only to note that the Duke and Duchess had stepped out and returned with admirable composure. Helena drew a steady breath, the tightness easing in her chest. For all she had dreaded the evening, it had proved—unexpectedly—pleasant; and, more unsettling still, she found she dreaded its end.

Chapter Fourteen

The letter arrived during breakfast. It was neatly folded and sealed with wax, but there was no identifying crest. Lucien's name was written upon the envelope, yet the hand was unfamiliar. He turned it over in his palm, weighing the paper as if its substance might betray its purpose.

"You look at that letter as if you fear it might bite you," Helena teased.

Lucien glanced slyly at her. His gaze dropped to her delicate hands—the right curled about a fork, the left a hair's breadth from her teacup. He remembered, too well, how those hands had felt wrapped about him at the ball the night before. He forced his thoughts elsewhere, lest he require another hurried retreat to some secluded corner.

He broke the seal and skimmed the contents. "Do you know a gentleman by the name of Mr. Finch?"

Helena stiffened, which was answer enough.

"I remember Mr. Finch," said Edmund.

"Oh?" Aunt Honora inquired.

Beatrice leaned forward, anticipation bright in her expression.

"He is a publisher," Helena said. "At first he agreed to print my manuscript, but after...my father's disgrace and the scandal with Lord Greene, Mr. Finch thought it best that we not proceed."

"That explains some of the other comments," Lucien said. "There are mentions of missing manuscripts, and of botanical illustrations being published without credit."

Helena's brow furrowed. "Who is the sender?"

Lucien caught the faintest tremor in her voice. Though her face appeared merely attentive, he suspected her feelings were more entangled than she would allow. "It is unsigned," he said. He turned the sheet again, examining the slope of the letters, the ink's thinness, the cramped, neat lines—nothing he recognised.

"How curious," Beatrice murmured.

"Indeed," Lucien said. "But we need pay no mind to idle gossip."

He had never received an anonymous letter before, yet he had an inkling who might have sent it. While the lines did not explicitly name Helena, they clearly pointed toward her. Someone wished to sow discord between himself and his duchess; he had no intention of permitting it.

"I do not like how the ton is talking about us," Aunt Honora said, eyeing him over her cup.

"They were already talking," Lucien returned. "At least, they will now say that I have a wife and cease their remarks about heirs."

Aunt Honora's lip curled. Her protests were growing tiresome. He was married to Helena; that would not change. It would be better if all concerned accepted the arrangement and laboured for peace, rather than endlessly quibbling.

He wondered if his aunt had sent the letter, yet another attempt to prove he had erred in choosing Helena. If not her, then Sir Bertram, eager to breed mischief before the assembly. The hand was too neat for his aunt; too affected for a steward; too cautious for a fool.

"You should try to find another publisher," Edmund said suddenly.

Helena stiffened afresh. She looked as if struck by lightning; her fingers tightened upon her fork. "Perhaps, someday."

Her tone was neutral, careful—as if she feared to loose the words into the room—yet he heard the small note of longing beneath.

Lucien's face softened. "You should."

Helena laughed lightly. "I have other concerns now."

"As well you should," Aunt Honora said. "The Greythorne Assembly quickly approaches. It would be unwise to remind the ton of your father's fall."

Helena's jaw tightened. "Of course, my lady."

"Afterwards," Beatrice said, brightening, "you may publish a handsome octavo with plates. I shall write a preface praising your genius."

"Beatrice," Aunt Honora warned.

"Why not? It would be delightful to have another lady-writer in the family," Beatrice persisted.

Lucien inclined his head. "Indeed. I think it would be."

His aunt cast him a weary look; he knew she nursed some sharp speech. A glance at Helena's gentled expression was worth any censure. He wanted his wife to be content. Helena was...

A respectable woman with many good qualities, and she deserved happiness.

When breakfast ended and the company dispersed, Lucien lingered a moment with the letter, holding it to the window's pale light. The paper was of middling quality; the wax common; the pen-hand disciplined but cautious. A coward's voice behind a curtain. He folded it once more and slid it into his pocket. If there were to be arrows loosed at his house, he would meet them at the door.

***

That evening, he entered his study and found it already occupied. He smiled wryly, leaning a shoulder against the doorframe. Helena, Edmund, and Meg were seated by the fire. Edmund and Meg played chess; Helena was curled in a chair with a book. He recognised a volume of Shakespeare's sonnets. Perhaps it was time to remove his papers elsewhere—or to rebuild the old study—for he could no longer pretend this room was entirely his own.

Lucien came forward. Edmund spied him first. "Your Grace!" he cried. "I am practising with Meg, so I may beat you next time."

Lucien chuckled. "Indeed? Such confidence."

Helena glanced up from her book. Meg rose and dropped a curtsy. He gestured for her to sit. "Who is winning?" he asked.

"Meg," Edmund said, a trifle sullen.

"Oh! I am not winning by much!" Meg declared, laughing. "It is still difficult to say who will triumph!"

Lucien bent over the board and found she had spoken true. The play was even, yet Meg's bishop stood in grave peril; if Edmund captured it, she would be in check.

"Do you wish to play, Your Grace?" Meg asked. "I am happy to yield you my chair."

Lucien rubbed his chin. Edmund's face brightened. "Will you play?"

"Yes," Lucien said.

The maid abandoned her seat, and Lucien took it. Meg stood behind Edmund, watchful as a general.

"Shall we reset the board?" Edmund asked.

"No," Lucien said. "We shall continue from here. Whose turn?"

"Yours, Your Grace," Meg replied.

Lucien whisked the bishop from danger and grinned. Edmund wrinkled his nose. "I was going to take that piece."

"Oh, I know," Lucien said, still grinning.

Behind her brother, Helena had abandoned Shakespeare, leaving the volume open upon her knee. They had scarcely been alone since the ball, and his pulse quickened at the recollection. Soon, they must speak of it. He would apologise for placing her in an uncomfortable, scandalous position, and assure her of his continued intention to defend her.

That would close the subject. He did not quite wish it closed. He had not sought intimacy with his duchess. He had entered this convenience with the intent of ignoring her until talk of heirs became unavoidable. Now, he doubted whether he wished to remain the distant husband. They were approaching something like friendship, which...

Presented certain dangers.

Edmund pushed a pawn; Lucien's attention returned to the board. There seemed no pressing reason for the move. Perhaps the boy wished only to reconsider his lines; perhaps he baited a trap. Good. Let him learn to think three moves hence.

Lucien advanced a pawn, keeping it safe from the knight. Edmund answered on the far file. They continued thus, testing one another—Lucien withholding the most obvious punishments, Edmund learning the angles and the weights.

"Finally!" Edmund exclaimed, laughing.

Lucien saw the danger too late and barked in amusement as Edmund captured his queen. "I did not even see it," he said. "Nicely done."

Edmund flushed at the praise. "Thank you, Your Grace."

Lucien studied the board anew. After a moment's consideration, he moved his knight. In three turns, he would have Edmund checkmated—assuming the boy did not perceive the snare.

Brow furrowed, Edmund slid his bishop. Behind him, Helena shifted; she was watching keenly now, Shakespeare forgotten.

Lucien moved his own bishop. "Check," he said.

Edmund frowned and stepped his king back to safety.

Lucien hesitated. He could draw out the game a little longer; yet he suspected Edmund knew he had erred.

"Oh no," Edmund gasped.

Their eyes met; he had seen it. "Would you like to reconsider that last move?" Lucien asked.

Edmund shook his head. "No. I wish to win because I am better. Not because you let me."

"Very mature of you."

Lucien swung his rook and secured the victory. "Checkmate."

Edmund sighed and tipped his king with one finger. "Almost."

"Almost," Lucien echoed. "You play very well. You may best me yet."

"Well played," Meg praised. "Very nicely done, Edmund."

"Yes," Helena said softly. "You nearly bested him."

"I shall work very hard to beat you, Your Grace," Edmund said.

Lucien chuckled. "No doubt you will. But perhaps we should do something else together. Will you join me in the stables tomorrow? We can ride."

He could not have said precisely what prompted the offer. Perhaps it was simply that Edmund was a boy, and boys liked riding and fencing and chess. Perhaps he remembered Henry's laugh in the saddle and could not bear a quiet house any longer.

Edmund's face brightened. "Really?"

"Of course."

"Thank you, Your Grace! I should like it very much."

"Excellent," Lucien said. "We ride after breakfast."

His gaze slid to Helena; she met it, expression unreadable. A shift, almost imperceptible, travelled between them; something wary, something warm.

"If you do not mind," he continued, "I should like to speak privately with your sister, Edmund. It is a marital matter."

Edmund looked between them and opened his mouth to object. "Now," Meg chided gently, "we must give them privacy."

Edmund nodded and rose. He bowed. "Your Grace."

Lucien inclined his head. In another breath, they were alone. Helena sighed and took up Shakespeare, holding the volume very tightly. "I suppose you wish to discuss the ball."

"I think we should."

"Do you?"

"I think I should apologise," he amended.

She shook her head. "Do not be absurd. I require no apology. I made my choice, and I knew what it meant."

Lucien studied her carefully. Her face was cool as ice, devoid of tenderness. "Do you?" he asked. "I would not have you think—"

"I also know what it did not mean," she said. "This is an arrangement, and it was—well—a matter of curiosity."

"Curiosity."

"Certainly. I had never handled a man like that before."

The rational part of him knew he ought to be relieved. Somehow, he was not. Perhaps it was only pride; even a man who rejects attachment resents being reduced to a diversion.

"I see," he said.

"Good." Helena deliberately returned her attention to Shakespeare.

He looked at her a long moment, feeling oddly as if he had been dismissed from his own study by a woman who deemed him no more than a curiosity.

"I always preferred John Donne."

She snorted. "There is no accounting for taste."

Lucien drew a volume of Donne from the shelf and opened to the cleverest of the poems. "Mark but this flea, and mark in this," he read, "How little that which thou deniest me is."

"I know that poem. Everyone knows that poem," Helena said. "And you are being denied nothing."

"The metaphor is exquisite. 'It suck'd me first, and now sucks thee, / And in this flea our two bloods mingled be—'"

"The expense of spirit in a waste of shame," she interrupted, "Is lust in action; and till action, lust / Is perjur'd, murderous, bloody, full of blame."

He knew that sonnet well. The margin bore his cramped notes on meter and rhyme, and his thoughts on Shakespeare's fierce rendering of desire. Had she chosen the poem by chance—or turned to it with the ball in mind?

"Savage, extreme, rude, cruel, and not to trust," she continued softly. "Enjoy'd no sooner but despised straight."

He cleared his throat. "Thou know'st that this cannot be said," Lucien read, "A sin, nor shame, nor loss of maidenhead."

Helena closed the volume with a sharp snap. "Shakespeare is the superior poet. You will not persuade me otherwise with Mr. Donne's elaborate, superfluous flea."

Lucien suspected they discussed more than poets. "I do not understand you," he said.

Worse—he was beginning to wonder if he understood himself.

Chapter Fifteen

Helena had not visited the library—which she would not think of as Lucien's study, for it was clearly a library—since their conversation about the ball. Yet her thoughts were all in disarray. Each day brought the Greythorne Assembly nearer. She would have to face Sir Bertram again.

Once, she had found refuge in the written word. She had pored over novels and poems, delighting in clever turns and elegant cadences. She meant only to secure a volume to pass the evening, and it was entirely by chance that she observed Mr. Peter Langford entering the library ahead of her.

She had nearly followed when the words that stopped her cold reached her ear. "Your Grace, there is something we must discuss, and I fear it concerns Her Grace."

Helena remained just within the door, fingers curled around its edge. Her heart rose to her throat. The room smelt of leather and ashes; a coal settled in the grate with a soft collapse. She could picture precisely where Lucien stood—the window, shoulders squared, that soldier's stillness he wore when displeased.

"Her Grace?" Lucien asked.

"Yes. I am not a man who enjoys trafficking in idle slander, but it is better that you hear of this matter from me than be caught unawares."

"I see."

A heavy pause fell, during which Helena scarcely dared to breathe. She ought to withdraw—or announce herself. If the matter involved her, she had a right to hear it. Yet if she revealed herself, Mr. Langford might speak with less candour;

men could be singular in their efforts to spare a lady's feelings. She remained where she was, as still and silent as the grave.

"There are anonymous letters circulating which malign Her Grace," Mr. Langford said.

"We received one," Lucien replied. "I would not say it maligned Helena so much as retailed unnecessary gossip. There was something about a missing manuscript."

Helena swallowed hard. He did not know the significance of the manuscript. Nor that she had stolen it. When Mr. Finch refused to return her work after declining to publish it, she had taken matters into her own hands. The manuscript was hers. It had been her right to reclaim it.

Mr. Langford sighed. "I fear some of these letters go beyond idle tattle. A few are decided in their malice—against you both."

"I see."

"There is talk that you have compromised the dukedom by allowing an unsuitable influence into your household. It is plain the 'unsuitable influence' denotes the duchess, and one letter names her directly."

Her face grew hot. An unsuitable influence, was she? She had been called worse by pens that fancied themselves sharp, but still, a well of frustration rose. Would the world not leave her be? Was a little peace so much to ask?

"Why is that a matter of concern?" Lucien said. "I did not anticipate everyone approving my marriage to Helena. What will they do? The thing is done."

"I am concerned what the gossip intends," Mr. Langford answered. "I fear someone seeks to discredit you, and with the Greythorne Assembly so near, your influence may be touched."

Lucien said nothing. Helena could almost see the vexed set of his brow—the weariness that drew at his shoulders when troubled. Guilt pricked. He must have known the risks in marrying her, but she did not wish her disgrace to harm him in any way.

"The Duke of Ravensgrave has long been the figure our landowners rally behind. Your forefathers were powerful before Parliament, and especially in those less formal labours where policy is born by degrees."

"I know it," Lucien said so softly she scarcely heard him. "But you also know I have never been the most political creature. I have not much head for negotiation."

"That is not true. You have a soldier's experience from Spain. Your officers and men esteemed you," Mr. Langford said. "That argues you can negotiate when there is need. You possess a certain charisma."

Spain? Officers?

Helena had not known he fought in the war. He must have returned upon his father's death to take the mantle of Ravensgrave. Had he ever wished it? She pictured him younger, sun-browned and straight-backed, delivering orders in some burning field while the smoke of another nation's ruin stained the sky. The image unsettled and steadied her at once.

"And the dukedom needs you to be a negotiator," Mr. Langford continued. "Your father left a tangle of investments. We must do nothing that would dissuade his partners from dealing with you. We must show the dukedom is steady—and that Her Grace is a benefit to all concerned."

"Is such a thing possible?" Lucien said hotly. "It appears the court of public opinion would hang her before hearing one sober fact. The whole affair is disgraceful. To drag a man's wife into these games—unseemly and absurd!"

Her breath caught. He defended her, despite everything. Helena's hands curled into fists; she drew away from the door. This was Sir Bertram's work. Of that she was certain.

She clenched her jaw and set a brisk pace for the gardens— the only sanctuary that never failed her. The cool wind brushed her cheek, familiar and bracing. The borders wore winter's threadbare livery; the yews kept their dark counsel. At the entrance to the rose garden, she spied Edmund, an apron clenched in his right hand, and Meg, their faces uneasy.

Her heart sank like a stone. "You look as though something is amiss."

"It is," Meg said, extending a folded paper. "Edmund found this in the garden apron."

Helena opened it. A neat, looping hand declared: *Your sister ruins everything she touches.*

Her breath hitched.

"Why would anyone say such a horrid thing?" Edmund cried. "It is untrue!"

Helena crushed the slip in her palm. "I am not surprised. I overheard Lucien with Mr. Langford. It seems there are many such malices in circulation."

"You must do something," Meg urged. "This note must have come from someone at Ravensgrave. You must learn who wrote it."

"To what end?" Helena asked. "If there are many letters abroad, unmasking one hand will not silence the rest."

"It will show that you will not endure insult," Meg returned.

Helena shook her head. "No. I shall burn this, and that is the end. Say nothing, Meg."

Meg drew a deep breath, displeased but obedient.

"Are you certain?" Edmund asked.

"Yes," Helena said. "My husband has cares enough without my tearing the household to bits to find a single slanderer."

"It is your household, too," Meg ventured.

Helena thrust the note into her pocket. "Nevertheless, I will leave it. Perhaps I shall change my mind; at present, there are better uses for my hands. I am in sore need of a distraction. Come, let us cut the roses back."

Neither argued, which was a mercy. Soon, Helena lost herself in the winter work—pruning and clearing what must give way. Thorns caught her glove; a bead of pain bloomed where the leather failed and pricked her skin. She thought of her mother's voice, teaching her to cut to a live bud and never be sentimental with dead wood. How simple a rule—and how mercilessly applicable to life. Her thoughts strayed to the manuscript tucked in her desk drawer. She had not touched it since she carried it out of Mr. Finch's shop. When she took it, she had nursed an ill-formed hope that she might one day publish; that she could mend what had been broken, restore her family's name. Foolish. Marriage had not solved her ills; she should have known it never could.

"Helena."

She tensed at Lucien's voice. Had he come to speak of letters? She steadied herself and rose, brushing earth from her skirts. "Yes?"

"I have received a notice from the council clerk," Lucien said. "Your presence is expected at the Greythorne Assembly."

"And? We had already thought that I should attend."

He inclined his head. Her eyes slipped to the letter in his hand. A stamp of the clerk's office sat squat and official in the corner; the paper had that stiff, officious rattle meant to overawe.

"Is something wrong, Your Grace?" Meg asked, drawing near. Edmund straightened from his careful work among the deadwood.

"We thought you would come as my guest," Lucien said. "It is now made plain you are to be a subject of inquiry. Sir Bertram has raised questions about your past, and many of the lords wish to see you for themselves."

Helena heard and understood—and yet dread spread like ice, for it confirmed what she had suspected. Sir Bertram again.

"My past is well known," she said. "It appeared in the scandal sheets. Why should this matter?"

"It does not," Lucien said tightly. "It is spectacle dressed as politics."

"If you will not defend my sister, she must defend herself!" Edmund burst out.

Lucien's gaze did not leave Helena's face. "I never said I would not defend her. She is my wife, and Sir Bertram seeks to ruin us both. We are allies in this."

The words threaded through her like warmth. He spoke not as a reluctant guardian of his name but as a man staking ground. She pressed her lips together, thinking. He had defended her before; she believed he would again.

"I will not insist you go," Lucien said. "These men have no right to interrogate you."

"But it will be harder for you if I do not. It will look as if I am hiding."

He smiled without mirth. "Do we care? It is not as though their opinion of you can sink further."

She bit her lip. He might be right; she foresaw no end to Sir Bertram's schemes. Yet she remembered Mr. Langford's warning—the investments, the habit of the countryside to take its cue from Ravensgrave. It did not sit well to have Lucien face them alone. "I will go with you," she said. "If I am to be judged regardless, I would rather meet it than hide. I am no coward, my husband."

"Very well, my wife." His voice was quiet, final. "Then we shall consider the matter settled."

He offered his arm; she did not take it, yet neither did she retreat. They stood a moment amid the cold perfume of bruised ivy and clean earth, the hush between them almost companionable.

Then, with a curt nod to Meg and a gentler one to Edmund, he turned back toward the house.

Chapter Sixteen

The carriage ride was long and quiet. Helena sat with her hands clasped in her lap, her temple pressed to the cold glass of the window. It was well past midday, yet frost still clung to the hills. The sky had turned prematurely dark, the sun concealed by bloated grey clouds. White fog rolled past in slow, unsettling waves, as if the world itself breathed.

"I fear the fog will worsen," Lucien said. "It is always worse over bodies of water."

"Water?"

He nodded. "There are several lakes along this road, many of them only a few miles from Sir Bertram's estate. I have instructed my driver to use his judgement. If the way grows unsafe, he will stop at the Owl & Nightingale. It is a respectable inn."

Helena did not argue. Despite her coat and the heavy furs, winter's lingering chill had sunk into her bones. An inn would be warm, at least.

They fell into silence again. Helena thought of Edmund and Meg, safe at Ravensgrave. She closed her eyes and longed to join them. Beatrice would be kind to Edmund, and Meg had good sense—more than a match for any schemes Lady Honora might contrive. The carriage creaked; the muffled splash of distant water came and went, swallowed by mist.

At last, the carriage slowed and stopped. Helena drew a deep breath and exhaled, misting the air. Gregory, the footman, opened the door. She and Lucien descended; he offered his arm.

She set her hand in the crook of his elbow and let him lead her to the inn—a modest timbered house furred with ice. Icicles pricked along the eaves; lantern-light burned like honey at the windows. When Gregory drew back the door, a wave of heat met her. Helena sighed, letting her gaze take in the room's golden firelight and dancing shadows, the murmur of low voices, the savour of roasted onions and ale. Lucien guided her to an empty chair by the hearth. "I shall arrange for supper, just the two of us."

"Thank you," Helena said, lowering herself into the chair.

As he moved away, she watched him. If she had been another sort of woman, she might have found something romantic in the prospect of sharing an inn's shelter. But she was not that woman.

She tipped her head against the cushions, looking idly into the flames. Some tension left her body, though not all. She could not forget what waited at journey's end. She imagined Sir Bertram's look, the ton's murmurs. She was going into a den of lions.

"Helena."

She blinked, only then realising she had fallen asleep. "Lucien?"

He inclined his head, a wry smile in his eyes. "Come. We shall take our supper in private."

He led her to a curtained alcove—a small table, two chairs, a candlestick with a steady flame. She sat opposite, conscious of the intimacy of the little chamber. Memory flashed: the ball, the heated recklessness of her hands upon him.

A maid arrived with their meal. It was simple fare—cold ham, a good loaf, and a thin white soup. She set down a dish of pickled walnuts and, last, a bottle of wine, offering an apologetic smile. "I beg you will pardon the plainness, Your Graces."

"That is to be expected," Helena said. "Thank you."

Lucien filled their glasses without comment, then turned his own, studying the dark surface. Helena took bread, savoured its warmth, dipped it into the soup, suddenly famished. After the cold road, even plain fare tasted heavenly. The wine was rustic but sound; it lit a little fire in her chest.

"Edmund is...something else," Lucien said at length.

"He is," Helena answered, curious.

"He puts me in mind of Henry as a boy. My brother was as lively as they come," Lucien said, a quiet chuckle escaping him. "We were a mischievous pair, forever making trouble for my father."

Helena had never heard him speak of his family. She sipped her wine and watched from beneath her lashes. There was a softness about him as he spoke of his youth, a light she had not seen before.

"Once we fenced in the parlour," he went on, smiling outright now. "We had heard of gentlemen who duelled in a drawing room and must needs reenact it. I broke a window."

Helena laughed in spite of herself. "I daresay your father was displeased."

"He was—utterly. And he blamed me for all of it," Lucien said, unrepentant. "Most unjust, since Henry was equally to blame. But Henry could do no wrong in his eyes."

"Did you ever resent him for it?"

He dipped bread, then shook his head. "No. Never. Everyone loved Henry. You would have loved him, too."

"You sound very certain."

"Because I am."

"You must miss him very much," she said gently.

His smile did not reach his eyes. "I do. It comes strangely. There are weeks when I hardly think of him at all." He paused, choosing his words. "Then there are moments when the longing takes me so strongly, I can scarcely bear it. It is the little things that undo me."

Helena nodded, a tight ache blooming in her chest. "I felt similarly when my father died. I did not weep in his study, nor among his books. But the sight of his old coat—" She broke off, swallowing. "That undid me every time."

They looked at one another, drawn together by grief's private recognition.

"What was he really like?" Lucien asked. "I have heard so much of Mr. Darrow. But—"

"He was not what they say," Helena said, the ache rising. "He was a brilliant man, and I believe in his work. They call him fraud and liar, but that is not the father I knew."

Lucien's expression softened. "I believe you."

She blinked, startled. "Why? I have given you no cause to do so."

"You have. I know you to be brilliant. That is cause enough."

Her breath shuddered. "You have no reason to think me brilliant."

"You wrote a book and had a publisher," Lucien said simply. "You would have been printed, had misfortune not intervened."

She took another swallow of wine. "That is kind."

"It is not kindness to speak truth," he said. "And I would have you know I shall defend you, whatever may occur at this assembly. You are my wife, and I am your husband. And—"

"And is that all?" Helena asked softly. "You will defend me because you must."

He frowned and finished his glass. When she reached for the bottle to refill it, her fingers brushed his. Warmth went through her, a small shock that ran straight to her core.

"No," Lucien said, his voice low and rough. "Not only that. I do like you, Helena. I may—may have begun to care for you. A little."

"Only a little?" she breathed.

"Yes."

A silence, not uncomfortable, settled. The candle guttered and righted itself; the fog pressed faintly at the panes. They finished the meal in companionable quiet, sharing the last heel of bread between them.

Afterwards, the innkeeper showed them upstairs. Helena inwardly winced as the key was set upon her palm.

"The lady's room," he said.

The lady's room.

The warmth banked in her chest. She was a wife with her own chamber. "Thank you," she murmured, her stomach turning.

Within, she pressed her back to the door and drew several steadying breaths. The room was clean, the fire bright. A basin and ewer stood ready; a bowl of withered lavender lent a faint sweetness to the air. It was entirely acceptable.

Yet unease traced her spine. She paced. The closeness in the carriage returned to her; the memory of that reckless night at the ball; the command of his hands and the unfathomable dark of his eyes. She remembered how he had watched her at supper, how his fingers had curved around the stem of his glass. Her breath quickened. That old ache returned between her thighs. It was agony to think of a man who had no notion what he did to her.

Before she could think better of it, she tore open the door—and nearly collided with Lucien. She gasped; he drew a sharp breath.

"I—came to ask if you needed more firewood," he said, composed again in a heartbeat; his hand was upon a small bundle of kindling.

Her thoughts scattered like a dropped glass. "Is this about...what happened last time?" she blurted.

A wash of colour rose to his cheekbones. His dark gaze was hard as polished stone. It took her a moment to understand the look; when she did, she faltered. "You are angry," she whispered. "With me?"

"I am not angry with you," he said. "It is everyone else. I am driven half mad, seeing you in public with those salacious rumours swirling. I cannot bear how little I can do. I would shield you if I could."

He stood very near—just as he had that night. Helena's breath shortened; his scent—clean, faintly spiced—rose to her senses.

"I do not need shielding," she said, lifting her chin.

"I know."

Hunger gathered within her. Her gaze dropped to his mouth. As if he felt the thought, he set the kindling aside and cupped her jaw—lightly, reverently—and heat flashed through her.

Then his mouth took hers. He kissed her deeply, fiercely; the rest of the world went still. She knew nothing and heard nothing but him. He consumed all she dared to feel.

He deepened the kiss; his hand slid to the nape of her neck. A low sound escaped her without leave. He kissed her again, hard and sure. Helena wound her arms about his neck and, with effortless strength, he lifted her. He carried her to the bed and set her upon it as if she were something precious, his gaze never leaving her face.

He broke the kiss to press his lips to her temple; his breath was hot upon her skin. "Tell me if you wish me to stop."

Her breaths came quick and unsteady. He kissed the line of her jaw, her throat. His hands trembled as he found the buttons of her pelisse; he undid them with care and drew the garment aside. He slid off her gloves, one by one, and brought her bare palm to his mouth, kissing the soft centre as if he paid homage. Helena pressed her thighs together and watched the firelight move over his features. He was so very handsome; words to send him away would not come.

A soft knock sounded at the door. Lucien stilled; his gaze flicked to the latch. "No," he said, low and dangerous. "They can wait." He crossed the room in two strides and set the bolt with a decisive click. The knock did not return.

He came back to her with the same implacable calm he wore at Ravensgrave when issuing orders. "Look at me," he said. She did. "I will not take what you do not freely give. But understand me, Helena—while I draw breath, no man touches you without answering to me."

His thumb traced the hollow at the base of her throat; her pulse leapt beneath it. "You speak like a tyrant," she whispered, shivering.

"I speak like your husband." His mouth brushed the place his thumb had marked. "Say stop, and I stop. Say stay, and I shall keep watch while you sleep. Or—" His hand slid to the fastenings of her bodice; the smallest pressure, a question. "Ask, and I will teach you how very much I can make you forget."

More than anything, she wanted his hands upon her—everywhere. Most of all, she wanted them where she ached. And if she let him, perhaps he would grant every wish she scarcely dared to name.

Chapter Seventeen

Lucien undressed her slowly, gently undoing the ties of her gown and letting it fall in a pool of fabric about her waist. She shifted from the bed and stood, taking a handful of the garment and tossing it onto the floor. He kissed her throat, and Helena reflexively tossed her head back, a low and guttural sound tearing from her throat. Her inner walls clenched, and her thighs quivered.

"So beautiful," Lucien murmured against her collarbone. "The most beautiful wife in the world—and mine."

She laughed at how absurd he was, how excessive the compliment, but her face still warmed with pleasure at his words. Lucien's hands swept over her breasts, her hands going to the laces of her stays. Helena's breath hitched, as he gently undid the ties.

"Are you certain about this?" she asked.

He kissed her neck in silent agreement as her stays fell away. Helena's body was taut with tension. No man had ever gazed at her with such bright intensity before. No man had ever touched her like this before, or seen her like this before.

She could tell him to stop. Perhaps she should have. They had agreed that their secret encounter at the ball meant nothing, but Helena...

This did not feel like nothing.

Did he notice her inexperience? If so, he said nothing. Soon, she was clad in nothing more than her shift. Helena shivered and curled her toes in anticipation.

Lucien lifted her shift and drew it over Helena's head in one sudden motion. An involuntary gasp tore from her as she stood

146

before him entirely naked. Lucien's gaze swept over her. His softness was gone, replaced instead with a heat greater than anything she had ever seen. "Beautiful," he said. "So beautiful."

He slowly removed his coat. Then, his jacket.

A lump rose in Helena's throat as she beheld him in his shirtsleeves. Her whole body trembled, and he looked at her as if she was the most beautiful woman in the world, as if he had never seen her equal.

Lucien slowly removed his shirt, and Helena beheld his bare chest. She scarcely dared to breathe, for she had only ever beheld such musculature in statues and paintings. Her fingers twitched at her sides, aching to trace the lines of his abdominal muscles and his broad chest. Helena's breath came in ragged gasps, marching in time with her own rapidly beating heart.

"Shall we?" he asked.

"Yes." She could not say precisely what she agreed to, but it seemed wondrous. "Please, Lucien."

"Lie down."

She lay back on the bed, and he lay beside her. Lucien smiled and caressed her stomach. Helena's muscles all tensed, and his hand drifted lower. He stroked the inside of her thighs, and a low, needy whine tore from her throat. Helena felt as though she was in her body and outside of it all at once. His fingers barely touched her, but even the smallest stroke of his fingertips sent jolts of pleasure coursing through her core.

If he moved his hand just a little lower, he would touch her there. Helena's breath caught. She was too aware of his dark eyes fixed upon the curls at the apex of her thighs.

"I almost wish that we had done this on our wedding night," he murmured. "I would have liked to have touched you then."

The ache between her legs grew, and she gasped. Helena's hips reflexively bucked, as if seeking his hand. Lucien chuckled under his breath. He touched her hips and gently brushed her curls. Helena took a steadying breath. "Please," she whispered.

"Please?" He arched an eyebrow. "What is it you want? Do you even know?"

She tossed her head back against the pillow, her chest heavy. Her nipples were pink and hard, like tiny rosebuds, and heat rushed to her face. No man had ever seen her so exposed before, and she found herself torn between the urge to preserve her modesty and to urge him to touch her in the place she desired him most.

After what seemed to be an eternity, his fingers drifted between her legs. She tensed as his thumb parted her curls and pressed hard against her. Helena gasped as he touched her centre.

"Are you all right?" he murmured.

Lucien was so concerned about her. A lump lodged itself in her throat. Since her father's death, Helena had felt as though she needed to care for everyone and to be everything. And he cared about her. He wanted her to be all right. She nodded.

His finger dipped lower, gently working her damp folds. Lucien's finger pressed against her entrance, and Helena's fingers curled tightly in the bed linens. She braced herself as he slowly pressed his finger inside her. Helena's inner walls pressed hard against him, jolting wildly around his digit.

He began to move his finger in and out, his gaze fixed firmly upon her face. A faint wet sound accompanied each movement, and Helena groaned. Tightness curled inside her stomach, building more and more with every heartbeat. She remembered this feeling from the night at the ball, when she had felt her body come alive.

Helena inhaled deeply, trying to adjust. "I—I feel..."

"Yes?"

She floundered for words. "I—I do not know how to describe it."

"A curiosity?" he teased.

Helena shook her head, a little laugh tearing from her. "More than that."

"Well. Here is something to court your curiosity," he said.

He shifted down the bed, his hands stroking her thighs. With a mischievous gleam, Lucien's head dipped between her legs. His tongue flicked against her core, and Helena shrieked in surprise. "No, you—you cannot possibly—"

He laughed, his breath puffing against her thigh. "I can," Lucien rumbled.

His lips lighted upon her core, and she jolted in surprise. Lucien grasped her hips, gently but firmly. His tongue pressed against her entrance, and Helena's toes curled. She groaned as the pressure grew in her stomach. Her thighs quivered. And there—

That rising feeling grew tighter and tighter within her. Helena's entire body shook, her hips and thighs moving without a single conscious thought. She groaned, writhing like a wild thing. Every lick and kiss and nip sent jolts of pleasure and anticipation coursing through her.

Then—

Without warning, the world seemed to halt. White spots obscured her vision, and she screamed as utter bliss overwhelmed her senses. Waves of pleasure crashed over her, and she all but collapsed onto the bed. Helena gasped for air, breathless and dazed from the force of all the sensations.

Lucien propped himself onto his elbows and gazed at her, a satisfied smirk crossing his face. "Did you enjoy that?"

"Yes," she breathed. "It was glorious."

Hesitation flickered in his eyes. He leaned over her and drew her in for a light, gentle kiss. "May I do more with you?" he whispered against her neck.

Helena did not trust her voice. Instead, she merely nodded.

"Are you certain?" he asked.

Helena sensed at once what he was really asking. She nodded again. "Yes. I am."

Lucien undid his trousers, revealing his already hard manhood. Helena swallowed hard. It looked as massive as it had that night at the ball, and she shivered, thinking about Lucien putting that inside her. To Helena, it seemed impossible for him to fit.

He positioned himself over her, and Helena clung to the bed linens as if her life depended on it. Lucien pressed against her entrance. There was a tightness, and she winced. Lucien paused. "Are you all right?"

He cared so much. "Yes," Helena whispered, grasping his arms. "Please."

Lucien entered her slowly, and her body pressed hard against him. He moved slowly within her, and the tightness slowly loosened. She clung to him, her nails digging into his shoulders as he rocked against her, pushing and pulling. He moved in and out, so very gently.

"You are doing so well," he murmured.

A ragged, feeble sound came from her throat. Helena was lost in the sensations, trying to put name to them all. She had not known that marital bliss would feel like this. She had never imagined that she might enjoy it, but she most assuredly did. Her body burned with want of him. Even as he drew himself in and out again, her heart beat in a silent song that reverberated inside her skull. More, more, more…

Her inner walls pulsed as Lucien moved more quickly. Helena caught the rhythm almost at once. They moved together. Sweat gathered at the small of Helena's back and behind her knees, as she and Lucien made love. That familiar ache bloomed within her, and she gasped.

Helena had the sensation of climbing higher and higher, and then—

Her legs quivered, and black spots obscured her vision. Waves of pleasure swept over her, drawing nearly breathless gasps from her trembling lips. Lucien drew her in for a kiss, and Helena moaned. She still felt him moving inside her, leisurely and gently.

His body shook, and she watched—fascinated and wanting—as Lucien gave a final shudder. Her husband's muscles all went tense, and a surge of wetness filled her. Helena's face warmed with the knowledge of what that meant, and she lay back, panting for air.

He traced his knuckles across her cheekbone and gazed at her with an unparalleled softness. Then, he slowly withdrew. Helena's eyes fell to his manhood, which was flaccid once more. That had been inside her. She shivered, equal parts anticipation and astonishment.

"You did very well," Lucien said softly. "You did not even bleed."

She started, eyes wide. "But I have never…"

Lucien arched an eyebrow and gave her a rakish smile. "I am in no doubt of your virtue," he said. "Some women do not bleed the first time."

She considered that for a moment. Lucien crossed the floor, and her eyes wandered shamelessly over his muscular upper back. The bliss from the amorous encounter had abated a little, and all the little doubts and questions began to emerge. She forced them down instead, indulging in her curiosity. He was an extraordinary specimen of manhood.

Lucien dressed. She watched in silence, aware of the damp heat still between her legs. After a moment, he went to the pitcher of water and wet a cloth with it. He returned to her and stood between her legs. "May I?"

She nodded. Lucien cleaned the proof of her arousal from between her thighs, his touch so gentle that she thought as if her heart might burst from the fondness blooming within her chest. She had never known this side of him, and she found herself liking this new facet of him.

"Thank you," she breathed.

He drew the cloth away and nodded. "I suppose we…" Lucien trailed off, his brow furrowing in uncertainty. "I suppose I shall dress you for bed, my sweet wife."

He held her shift, and she shyly stood, letting him dress her. As Lucien smoothed the material over her waist and hips, a little fissure of excitement bloomed within her. His hands lingered for longer than was necessary, steady and warm against her skin. "Good night," he said after a heartbeat.

Lucien pulled her against him, embracing her tightly and tenderly. A shiver traced the path of her spine. He released her almost at once.

"Good night," she echoed.

Still, he lingered. When he turned away, it seemed as though it took an eternity for him to reach the door. He paused for a moment and cleared his throat. "Try not to worry overly," Lucien said. "I know that these men at the Greythorne Assembly will be vicious. Just know that you have nothing to fear from them. I will not let them cause you any harm."

"I know."

He gave her a final smile and closed the door behind him. Helena took a shaky breath of air and fell back against her bed linens, her mind awhirl with everything that she had just felt and done. She was suddenly wonderfully tired.

Chapter Eighteen

They arrived after sunset. The estate was lit, its flickering lamplights like stars brought to earth against the dismal grey of winter. Flags bearing the family crests of the invited families were hung across the open gates. Lucien inhaled sharply, noting the conspicuous absence of the Ashmore banner. Sir Bertram had never understood the art of subtlety.

Lucien glanced at Helena to see if she noticed anything amiss. Her expression betrayed nothing. She had been quiet since their amorous encounter. Lucien regretted it but feared her honest answer too much to ask. "We are here," he said, as though that were needed.

Where else would they be?

"I suppose it is too late for us to turn away and go elsewhere," Helena said dryly.

"I am afraid so."

It was a wonderful fantasy, though. Lucien dared to imagine simply calling for the driver to halt and going elsewhere. Perhaps, they would return to Ravensgrave and spend the evening in the conservatory together. If he were very fortunate, he might persuade her to indulge in another amorous encounter. His blood quickened at the thought.

The carriage came to a halt. There were no other carriages before the grand house, no one coming or going. "It seems as though we are the last to arrive," Lucien mused.

They left the carriage, and Lucien offered his arm. Helena placed her hand on his elbow, and a shiver of delight rushed through him. He remembered that same delicate hand wrapped around his desire. It was an entirely inappropriate thought, especially given the solemn occasion, but since their dalliance in the inn, he found himself thinking more and more about how much his body wanted hers.

Just as they reached the door, it burst inward. A flustered-looking butler stared at them with wide eyes. "Y-Your Grace!" he exclaimed.

Lucien blinked, taken aback by the force of that unpolished greeting. "It is, indeed. I am here for the assembly."

The butler cleared his throat. "The assembly has already begun, Your Grace."

"Already begun?" Lucien asked. "It is not set to begin until tomorrow morning."

"Sir Bertram suggested that the assembly begin earlier today," the butler said, his face now impossibly red. "There were no objections to his request."

Beside Lucien, Helena inhaled sharply.

"I see," Lucien said.

What else could he say? He fought back the impulse to argue, for he knew that it would accomplish little. This butler was not the cause of his vexation, and any furious reaction would only reflect poorly on him. It was quite clear that this slight was intentional, though. Lucien clenched his jaw, thinking.

"Should we..." Helena trailed off uncertainly.

"We will join them," Lucien said. "I imagine the assembly is being held in the great hall."

"It is," the butler said, seeming to regain his composure. "I can lead you there, Your Grace."

"That would be wonderful," Lucien said, turning to Helena. "Do you wish to join me? You could go elsewhere if you desired."

Helena bit her lip, clearly torn. It would be easier for her to flee and prolong the inevitable meeting with the men of the assembly. Lucien felt a similar impulse, but he was a duke. He did not have the luxury of hiding, even for a little while.

"I will stay with you," Helena said. "Why delay the inevitable?"

Lucien forced a smile. "Because it is unpleasant, of course."

She squeezed his arm, and he patted her hand. If he had to face the assembly, at least he had such a resolute and formidable woman at his side.

The butler led them to the great hall, two footmen snapping to attention and throwing open the doors. Sir Bertram's great hall was a large room made of white marble, warmed by the flickering firelight. A massive rosewood table sat in the centre of the room, all its seats filled save one.

Lucien supposed that was his own, although his father had never sat there. He had sat in the centre, in the seat presently occupied by Sir Bertram. Lucien clenched his jaw. Once, these men had been his father's allies. They had been his allies, his acquaintances, and friends. As the gentlemen and their wives noticed his presence, their conversations died. Silence reigned.

Sir Bertram stood fluidly. "Your Grace," he said, bowing. "Welcome! I hope you will forgive me for suggesting that we begin the assembly a little early, but it seemed...a dreadful waste to delay when all, save one of us, were already present."

"I see," Lucien said, imbuing those two words with every ounce of displeasure he could.

"I shall be certain to make you aware of everything that has already been said. There has been considerable conversation about influence, especially when changes in households may compromise a vote," Sir Bertram said. "And of course, such changes are of concern to us all. Ill-thought votes and alliances here might well be reflected in parliamentary dealings."

Helena had not been mentioned by name, but it was clear to Lucien that she was the influence. Lucien steeled himself. Sir Bertram was certainly a brazen man! But how had he convinced these other gentlemen to agree with his schemes?

"Would you like to take your seat?" Sir Bertram asked.

"I notice there is no seat for my wife," Lucien said.

Sir Bertram's easy smile never wavered. "An unfortunate oversight. I had thought that Her Grace might wish to rest after such a long journey. We have long been acquainted with one another, as you know."

"I am not tired," Helena said. "I wish to stay."

"Then, I will stand beside her," Lucien said. "There is no need to delay the proceedings any longer."

***

I suppose I should be grateful that I was given a seat, Helena thought, as she sat for dinner.

However, given that she was seated far from Lucien and surrounded by unfamiliar people, Helena was not entirely certain that being forced to stand presented a worse fate. Her eyes drifted to Sir Bertram, laughing merrily at someone's remark. Doubtless, he was the architect of this illogical seating arrangement.

To Helena's right was Lady Huws, a stately widow and Sir Bertram's distant cousin. Even Helena, who knew so few of the ton, knew of the lady's penchant for gossip. As if she sensed Helena thinking of her, Lady Huws cleared her throat. "Miss Darrow," she said.

Helena bristled at the address, wondering if it was an intentional insult. "Yes?"

"We are all terribly curious to know about your marriage," Lady Huws said, her green eyes bright. "What is it like being married to such a secretive man?"

The other ladies, who were seated nearby, did not pause in their conversations, but Helena felt their attention drift to her. Heads and glances tilted slightly in her direction. Even though the room was filled with sound, there was the strange sensation of the space holding its breath.

"I suppose it is like any other marriage," Helena said at last. "How well does any woman really know her husband before marriage?"

Lady Huws laughed. "You must have more thoughts than that."

Helena shook her head and took another spoonful of soup, hoping that she might avoid some of the questions by focusing her attention on the food instead. It was a ridiculous thought, which she knew, but desperation rose tightly in her chest.

"You must be delighted, though." A dark-haired woman with pale eyes gestured further down the table—to Lucien—with her glass of wine. "After all, it is not every naturalist's daughter who can marry a duke."

Someone muttered something that sounded like disgraced daughter, but the words were pitched too lowly for Helena to identify a speaker. If the words had not resulted in a titter of laughter, she might even have thought she had imagined them.

"I find your courtship charming," Lady Huws said.

She made *charming* sound profoundly like an insult.

"I suppose the third suitor was the best one," a lady murmured. "I am surprised His Grace agreed to marry her at all, given…"

Helena did not need to hear the rest to know that the lady implied Lord Greene's death was Helena's fault. Her eyes drifted to Lucien. Even across the space, their gazes met. Helena took a steadying breath. It was only dinner. She just had to endure until the meal was finished. Then, she could have the solitude of her thoughts or Lucien's company. Either would be welcome.

"How is Ravensgrave?" another lady asked. "Is it true that the estate was nearly destroyed by a fire?"

"Some of it." Helena offered nothing else.

That was how she passed most of the dinner, answering only the questions that were asked of her and with as little information as possible. After what felt like an eternity, the meal ended. She knew that the ladies would gather together to have tea and gossip, but at least she had overcome one ordeal.

"Your Grace."

A young woman with thick, auburn hair appeared at her side. Helena did not know her name, but she vaguely recognized her as one of the ladies who had been seated in the great hall near Sir Bertram.

"I feel that there is something you should know," she said, tilting her head towards a small alcove, which offered some semblance of privacy.

A weariness crept into Helena's bones, for she knew instinctively that no good could come from a private conversation. Still, she followed the woman, whose eyes darted about as if she feared that the very walls might have ears of their own. They stepped through a door, leading into the gardens. Hissing between her teeth at the bitter cold, Helena pulled a shawl tightly about her shoulders. The air was damp with chill, and miserable.

"I do not wish for us to be heard," the woman said. "I suppose it would be more proper to wait for an introduction, but...well. I am Lady Alwood. It is a pleasure to make your acquaintance."

"Likewise," Helena said, furrowing her brow. "What do you want from me?"

"To warn you. Before your arrival, Sir Bertram submitted a formal motion to disqualify His Grace's votes from the assembly on the grounds of 'moral entanglement.'"

Helena's stomach churned. "Moral entanglement?"

Lady Alwood nodded. "I know that you may not understand the significance of all this. You are not one of this circle."

Helena bit back an instinctive retort, for this woman—a rarity among the other ladies—did not speak as though Helena ought to be ashamed for not being one of them. Without asking, it was impossible to know why this lady was willing to aid her efforts. Helena felt a little less alone, knowing that even just one of those noblewomen might be sympathetic to her plight.

"It matters," Lady Alwood continued. "Influence matters."

"I understand."

Lady Alwood nodded. She hesitated for a heartbeat, giving Helena a sharp glance. "I do not know you, but...as a woman who once survived a scandal, I feel that I should warn you. Sir

Bertram's ally Lord Adlington has mentioned that he has some outside sources who are prepared to discredit you more directly."

Helena's blood ran cold. "Do you know anything about them?"

"I believe a publisher was mentioned."

"Finch."

"Yes. He was mentioned briefly. There may have been more names."

That did not entirely make sense to Helena. Mr. Finch had once agreed to publish her manuscript, but that was her only connection to the man. She could not think of anything he might know about her that would be especially condemning. Even if Mr. Finch had surmised that she had taken back her manuscript, it had been hers. It was not something which he could expect to garner sympathy with.

"I must go," Lady Alwood said. "Just—take care."

"Thank you," Helena said.

The lady smiled and retreated inside the house. Helena remained in the gardens for a moment longer, watching her breath frost the air. This situation had worsened so quickly, and it was all her fault. If Lucien had never married her, he might still have influence. He would not need to fear men like Sir Bertram.

Helena closed her eyes and sighed deeply. Her fingers were going numb. She turned around and slipped back into the house, nearly colliding with Lucien.

"Helena," he said.

"I was speaking with Lady Alwood," she said without preamble.

Lucien raised an eyebrow. "Another scandalous lady," he said wryly.

"And she found a scandal."

Helena quickly told him what Lady Alwood had said, Lucien's expression growing harder with every word. Once Helena finished, he clenched his jaw and stared at her for a long moment. "We are leaving," he said sharply. "This very moment."

"We cannot," Helena said. "That is precisely what Sir Bertram wants. We must stay."

Lucien ran a hand through his hair. "You are right," he muttered, "but I do not like it."

"Nor do I."

"It will only be a few days."

"Yes," Helena agreed. "You must try to regain as much influence as you can during that time."

Lucien nodded. Without warning, he pulled her into a tight hug, and his warmth shuddered through her. "I will come see you later. Take care of yourself, Helena."

"You, too."

He released her, and Helena ached for his warmth. Lucien's eyes flitted in the direction of the council chamber. "Well," he said. "Once more into the breach."

"Not Shakespeare's best," Helena said.

He winked. "No. Not at all."

Without another word, he walked to the council chamber, leaving Helena alone with her damp shawl and a tempest of thoughts.

Chapter Nineteen

Mr. Langford joined them early the next morning. After breakfast, Helena and Lucien had retreated to Lucien's rooms to have some small measure of privacy before they were forced to join the rest of the ton. Coldness filled Helena when she thought of their stares, questions, and whispers. Even the brief hope Lady Alwood had brought was not enough to rouse enthusiasm for the day.

"How bad is it?" Lucien asked.

He and Helena sat across from one another, warmed by the crackling fire. If Helena closed her eyes, she could almost pretend that they were at Ravensgrave together and that there were no schemes to counter.

Mr. Langford withdrew a folded scrap of paper and handed it to Lucien. "It could be worse, Your Grace."

"Such optimism," Lucien said dryly.

From where she sat, Helena could not read the paper even if she craned her neck. Mr. Langford clasped his hands behind his back and smiled sheepishly. "It seems worse than it is. I promise."

Lucien sighed.

"What is it?" Helena asked.

"It is a list of expected votes." Lucien tilted his head towards Mr. Langford. "I do admire how quickly you obtained this information."

"Thank you," Mr. Langford said.

"Five names already lean away from Sir Bertram," Lucien said. "That is promising."

164

"How many votes do you need?" Helena asked.

She had not thought to count how many noblemen were present at the assembly.

"Eight, but we want to be cautious. Lord Summerton is leaning away from Sir Bertram, but he is a notoriously fickle man. It is possible that he—or one of the others—might change their vote," Mr. Langford replied. "Fortunately, we do have two noblemen who might shift in our direction."

"Who?" Lucien asked.

Hope stirred in Helena's chest.

"Lord Hazelton and Lord Aderwell," Mr. Langford said.

Lucien frowned, his intense gaze fixed on the list in his hand. "Lord Hazelton will vote however his wife thinks he ought to."

"Really?" Helena asked.

"Yes," Lucien said. "It is well-known that she is the true power behind the earldom. She is a force to be reckoned with. I daresay that she puts my aunt Honora to shame with the strength of her will."

"Lady Aderwell is similarly influential," Mr. Langford said. "If you can persuade the ladies that their husbands ought to vote against Sir Bertram, they will."

Lucien frowned. "I do not know if I trust myself to persuade two ladies. It will seem…"

"Like you are trying to gain their favour?" Mr. Langford guessed wryly. "Yes. Precisely like that."

"Perhaps, I can do it," Helena said.

Lucien looked doubtfully at her, and a little spark of hurt flickered inside her chest.

"Why do you hesitate?" Helena asked.

"I do not want to see you hurt," Lucien said. "These people cannot be trusted, and they have spent the past day gossiping maliciously about you."

"Not all of them," Helena said. "Lady Alwood has proven herself to be an ally. There may be others."

"Lady Alwood has allied herself with you?" Mr. Langford asked.

"Yes," Lucien said.

Helena briefly explained what had occurred, and after she finished recounting the encounter with Lady Alwood, Mr. Langford gave her a shrewd look. "Lady Alwood also suffered a scandal as a young woman. She may sympathize with your situation."

"What was the scandal?" Helena asked.

"She married below her station," Lucien said.

"Yes," Mr. Langford said. "Her first husband was a solicitor."

Helena blinked, a little startled. "Was that Lord Alwood?"

"No," Lucien replied. "She married again after her first husband died."

Helena leaned forward a little. "What about the other ladies? Lady Hazelton and Lady Aderwell? Do they have any scandals in their pasts? Anything that might make them sympathetic to our situation?"

Mr. Langford shook his head. "I am unaware of any."

Helena bit the inside of her cheek. "I want to try, though. If those ladies are so powerful and influential, they might also be more enlightened than most."

At any rate, she had to try.

***

Around midday, Helena changed into her best gown. It was a recent addition to her wardrobe, a green silk gown with ivy embroidered at the cuffs. The garment was elegant and fashionable, and she felt like a proper duchess wearing it. She silently prayed that was enough to make her persuasive to the ladies Hazelton and Aderwell.

She entered the drawing room and found it filled with noblewomen, cousins of landowners and political wives, many of whom appeared—to Helena's eyes—as though they were feigning disinterest in the events around them. A lump rose in her throat. Lucien and Mr. Langford had described the ladies to her.

She searched the crowd for Lady Hazelton, who had a distinctive beauty mark on her cheek and black hair, and Lady Aderwell, who was fair-haired and uncommonly tall for a woman. After a few moments, she found a tall, slender woman with fair hair. She stood taller than the others. Helena hurried across the drawing room, a bright smile on her face.

"Lady Aderwell," she said.

The fair-haired woman turned her head and fixed her with a sly look. Helena sighed in relief. She might have died of embarrassment if she had been wrong about the lady's identity. "The infamous Duchess of Ravensgrave. Your reputation precedes you."

"As does yours."

Lady Aderwell tilted her head back, smiling. Helena noted that the few other women, who remained clustered around Lady Aderwell, were mostly silent. They watched her interaction with Helena as if it were the most fascinating conversation they had ever seen.

Helena straightened her spine. For better or worse, something about Lady Aderwell reminded her of Lady Honora. "I have heard that you are a woman who always speaks her mind," Helena said.

Lady Aderwell arched an eyebrow. "How brazen! I see that you certainly always speak yours."

"I had hoped to speak to you about Sir Bertram's suggestion—that Lucien's votes be dismissed."

Lady Aderwell hummed, her face shifting into a look of mock surprise. "And what do you propose that I do about it?"

Helena tried to decide if the truth would help or hinder her cause. "I thought you might persuade your husband to support mine," she said, deciding on honesty. "I am told that he greatly values your thoughts on political matters."

She suspected that Lady Aderwell would notice a lie, so it was best not to test her luck. Maybe she could win the lady's goodwill with honesty. "How is supporting His Grace to my benefit? Or my husband's?"

"Our friendship and support in your endeavours," Helena said. "Lucien is a great man, and I am proud of the Ravensgrave that we are building together. To continue improving the dukedom, Lucien needs his influence, and he should not be punished for marrying me."

"Why not?" A dark-haired woman joined them. Helena's eyes darted to the beauty mark on the woman's cheek.

"Your husband most certainly knew the consequences of marrying you," Lady Hazelton said.

Helena inclined her head, acknowledging the point. She was trying to find a good rebuttal. After floundering for a heartbeat, she sighed softly. "Perhaps, he did know. That does not mean this treatment is fair. I know that there are scandals tied to my name, but that—that should not affect Ravensgrave and the people living there. We should not allow petty grievances and old scandals to dictate how we take care of our tenants or each other."

"I have heard that Ravensgrave is half in ruins," Lady Aderwell said.

"It is," Helena said. "Due to several misfortunes that have befallen Lucien. It is no reflection on his character or what he might accomplish if he is but given the opportunity."

Lady Alwood shifted forward and touched Helena's wrist. "Most of us have experienced some misfortune, due to no fault of our own. You are quite right. Just because that is how things are does not mean the world should be like that."

"It is more difficult for ladies," Lady Aderwell mused. "Our sins remain with us for much longer than men's do."

"Regrettably," Lady Hazelton said.

"And we are expected to be perfect," Helena said. "If we do anything that is not explicitly proper, it is as if we have committed some unforgivable thing."

"Yes," Lady Aderwell said. "I do not think there is any lady here who would disagree."

"Indeed," Lady Alwood said, offering Helena a small smile.

"Then, will you help me?" Helena asked softly. "Will you help me restore Ravensgrave to its former glory?"

"My husband is the one who votes," Lady Aderwell said coyly. "But I promise to try."

And that was all Helena could reasonably ask for.

***

As she returned to Lucien's private parlour, Helena pulled her gloves free and tossed them lightly onto the nearby table. Lucien had spent the evening speaking with the other lords of the ton. During the evening, they had both returned to the room.

Lucien sat by the fire, Mr. Langford seated to his right. Together, they looked over a handful of papers and a small book filled with cramped handwriting. Helena spied the names of several lords along with notes about what they had voted on in the past.

Lucien glanced up at her. "Were you able to find the ladies?"

"Yes," Helena said.

Noting Lucien's furrowed brow and the empty glass at his side, Helena took the decanter of brandy and carefully filled it. Her husband glanced at her, his expression softening just a little.

"I believe our conversation went well," Helena said.

She briefly recounted what she had discussed with the other ladies, Lucien, and Mr. Langford, listening in silence. "Good," Lucien said once she was finished. "Hopefully, they are able to persuade their husbands to act against Sir Bertram."

"We shall see," Mr. Langford said. "I would feel better about the situation if we could get a few more votes on your side, Your Grace."

"Agreed," Lucien said, raking his hand through his hair. "I believe that is everything that I need from you today, Langford. Thank you for your help with this matter."

Mr. Langford stood and bowed, his expression soft with sympathy. "Always a pleasure, Your Grace. If I can be of any more assistance, do not hesitate to ask."

"Of course," Lucien murmured absentmindedly.

After Mr. Langford had gone, Helena drew her chair nearer to her husband. He looked so distressed that her heart ached. She tentatively reached for him, her fingertips brushing his sleeve. Perhaps, she could smooth some of the fears that held him.

Perhaps, they could explore what they had in the inn or discover something new about themselves. A softness swept over her, and her lips slightly parted, as she tried to find the best words to say.

"It is getting late," Lucien said.

She froze.

Lucien stood and moved to the window, seemingly oblivious to her attempt at something almost affectionate. "We need to sleep," he said. "The hour grows late, and I imagine tomorrow will be worse."

"Worse?" she asked.

"Yes. Good night, Helena."

She stood in the middle of the room for a long time before retreating to the bedchamber. Helena took a shuddering breath, her hands shaking as she unfastened her dress.

Lucien had rejected her. Did he regret that night at the inn? Helena's heart hammered against her ribs, so violently that she thought she might be ill.

Or worse, did he regret marrying her at all?

Chapter Twenty

The vote was held early in the morning. That was both a blessing and a curse. Lucien had never enjoyed the morning, and he preferred not to do business at such an early hour. His dismal mood was worsened by the crowded hall, the heat of bodies, and the noise that rose around him like a wave. Everything was too formal and loud.

His eyes searched the gallery. There was Helena, looking lovely in a pink silk gown, with Langford beside her. Lucien swallowed hard and tried to force his nerves to calm. It was time.

He cleared his throat. "I wish to speak on land reforms," he said. "Specifically, the Dukedom of Ravensgrave and the surrounding areas."

He had practiced what he would say so often that he had nearly memorized the words. Still, his heart seized as the noise quieted, everyone watching him. Sir Bertram's face was infuriatingly polite.

Lucien had to remember that five names had sided against Sir Bertram. If Helena had succeeded, he might have seven names.

Eight, including his.

"I know that certain parties have sought to besmirch my reputation," Lucien said. "Vicious rumours have been spread about my wife. I will not address these accusations, for doing so would detract from the purpose of our gathering here today, which is to form alliances in anticipation of springtime when parliament meets once again. As many of you know, I have a plan to improve roads throughout Yorkshire, which will allow trade to flow more smoothly between our estates. My changes will not only bring us together but also help our tenants during difficult times."

Lucien took a deep breath. His eyes darted to Sir Bertram, who continued to smile insipidly.

At his speech's end, the table came to life with arguments and disagreements. Lucien clenched his jaw, scarcely daring to breathe. His mind mentally recalled the five names. Each time one of those names spoke in his favour, he let himself breathe a little more easily.

At last, it was time for the vote. It passed.

Sir Bertram cleared his throat and stood. "Before we agree to all support this plan in the spring, I think we ought to vote on if His Grace's vote even counts. While he was quick to dismiss the scandals surrounding his name, that does not mean we should. We all know about the immoral choice that he has made."

Lucien's face grew hot. It was obvious to everyone that Sir Bertram was talking about Helena. Lucien had a wild thought of challenging the man to a duel for Helena's honour, but he knew to his core that such a reckless action would only serve to worsen the problems swirling around him.

Lucien cleared his throat and stood, smiling tightly. "While I respect your concern, your fears are entirely unfounded, Sir Bertram. My wife is a good woman who cares deeply about the improvement of Ravensgrave, whose heart is filled with love and passion. These rumours are nothing more than salacious attacks meant to tear apart a good woman."

"I know it can be difficult to believe the truth," Sir Bertram said tightly.

The man's eyes flicked to the gallery, where Lucien knew the man was looking at Helena.

The vote began, and Lucien scarcely dared to breathe. The five names were still on his side. Lucien's vote made six.

Lord Hazelton paused and glanced at Lucien for a long time. After a beat, Lord Hazelton shook his head. He disagreed with Sir Bertram.

One more vote. They only needed one more, and they would have succeeded.

When it was agreed that Lucien's votes would be counted, he withheld a sigh of relief. Colour rose to Sir Bertram's face. It took all the strength of Lucien's will not to smirk in response.

"I would like to vote again," Sir Bertram said.

The disagreement was swift and merciless.

Lucien glanced at the gallery and saw Helena smile. His pulse jumped a little. They had won. It was certain to be a fleeting victory, but it was a victory nonetheless.

A few noblemen shifted uncomfortably in their seats, but the vote would stand. Most of the room had agreed that Lucien's votes would be counted, and most of them had agreed to support his land reforms. It was the best possible outcome given the situation.

After the assembly ended, Sir Bertram was the first man to flee the room. He all but shoved past several other peers in his haste to escape.

Coward, Lucien thought.

He looked up at Helena, who smiled tentatively at him. There was something distant in her expression that he did not understand. Maybe it was being so close to Sir Bertram once again. Lucien sighed, forcing a smile as a nobleman congratulated him.

Soon, he and Helena would be back at Ravensgrave, and Sir Bertram would be a minor inconvenience, lost quickly to the mists of time and more recent scandals.

***

They left the estate at noon. Langford remained behind to finalize the estate papers. Lucien and Helena sat in the carriage together. It was quiet. The first hour passed in aching stillness. Outside the window, the countryside was grey and wet, blurred through the thin pane of glass.

Across from him, Helena sat with her back straight and her gaze distant. He tried not to stare, but his eyes seemed to keep finding her. Lucien's gaze swept over the line of her delicate jaw, her cheekbones, and her lovely eyes. She looked fragile, like something precious that must be handled very delicately, and yet he knew that she was something more.

Helena had borne all those scandals before ever meeting him, and she had done it without the benefit of his title and status. How hard it must have been! There was a strange pull inside him, some strong and nameless sensation that tugged at him and drew him in.

What did it mean?

By the time the carriage halted before Ravensgrave, Lucien still did not have his answer. Helena only met his eyes once they reached the front steps. She stumbled just a little on the wet stone, and Lucien grasped her elbow, keeping her upright.

She gasped sharply. "Thank you."

He slowly let his hand trail down her arm, even that slight touch sending a jolt of lightning surging through his body. Helena was really something quite remarkable.

The door was opened, and sound burst in Lucien's ears. "Helena!" Edmund exclaimed, all but throwing himself at his sister.

She embraced him back, and something stirred vaguely within Lucien, seeing her kindness. Someday, Helena would make an excellent mother. His breath caught in his throat.

Meg joined them, smiling brightly. "How was the journey?"

"Pleasant," Helena said.

That answer left out so many details, and Lucien did not fault his wife at all for neglecting to mention all the complications at the assembly.

"You are back!" Beatrice exclaimed, hurrying down the staircase. "Oh, finally! I had the most marvellous thought while you were away! We should host a literary salon here at Ravensgrave! The setting would be just splendid!"

Only Aunt Honora was absent, but Lucien knew better than to expect sentiment from her. She would go about her day as if there was nothing amiss, and she would happen into him when they crossed paths. Not a moment before.

That might be for the best, given that he had so much to think about: Sir Bertram's schemes, Helena, and his own strange feelings. He darted up the stairs, not exchanging a word with anyone, and left all the joyous reunions to his wife.

***

London greeted Sir Bertram with sheets of rain that lashed against the windows of the carriage. He grimaced. Given the disaster that had been the Greythorne Assembly, the weather seemed appropriate. Bertram had a plan, though.

He stepped from the carriage and entered the side office of a publishing house. After learning that this publisher had

Helena's manuscript, some ridiculous botanical text, Bertram had decided to fund the publisher himself. At first, he had only intended a little sabotage. The publisher was losing money, and he had offered a solution to their problems. Bertram would fund the publishing house in return for Finch agreeing not to publish Helena's manuscript.

But after learning that she had married Ashmore, Bertram had realized that this publisher might prove more useful than he had initially thought.

"Good evening," Bertram said curtly.

Finch waited behind a desk. His mouth pressed into a thin, disapproving line, but he said nothing contrary. He never did. Finch was a rather cowardly man, something that Bertram had cheerfully noted during their first meeting.

"I have something that I would like for you to publish," Bertram said. "A pamphlet. I want it to be spread throughout all of Britain. Spare no expense."

Finch cleared his throat. "Of course, sir."

Bertram withdrew the damp papers from his coat and placed them firmly on the desk. The title *The Ashmore Marriage & the Woman Who Broke Her Patron* loomed in bold, dark handwriting. Below it was the account of Helena's entire life. A version of it, anyway.

Finch peered at the text and hissed between his teeth. "Ashmore," he said.

"A political rival," Bertram said flippantly. "No one that you need to worry about, of course."

Finch frowned and read the paper upside down. Bertram caught the flare of recognition in Finch's eyes when he saw Helena's name. "Now," Bertram said, choosing to dissuade any disagreement before it could be voiced. "Remember that I own your little shop. I do not ask for much from you—just this one pamphlet."

"But Miss Darrow..." Finch trailed off.

"I am going to give Miss Darrow everything that she deserves," Bertram said hotly.

And he would. Ashmore might have ruined Bertram's plans to seize power at the Greythorne Assembly, but Bertram had never been a man to give ground easily. Ashmore had won a battle. That was all.

Bertram would win the war. Not only would he strip Ashmore of influence, but he would also have his vengeance on Helena, who had rejected him.

"I just...she is—she is a duchess now," Finch stammered.

Bertram raised a cool eyebrow. "And? Do not grow a conscience now. It does not suit you."

Finch swallowed hard.

"I will return for these in a week," Bertram said.

Then, he turned on his heels and stepped back into the merciless rain. When Bertram had the pamphlets in his possession, he knew precisely where the first few would be sent. He smiled to himself as he climbed into his carriage. Poor, naïve Helena had no idea the storm that he was about to unleash upon her.

Chapter Twenty-One

Helena held the pamphlet with shaking hands. It had arrived with the day's post with no indication of who the sender might be. The Ashmore Marriage & the Woman Who Broke Her Patron was printed boldly across the front page. For several seconds, Helena's breath seemed to stop. Her chest tightened.

She had some inkling of what the pamphlet might say, but still she tore it open with the smouldering, desperate hope that its contents might be concerned with any other woman in Britain.

This pamphlet details the cruel machinations of an infamous young lady, with whom most of the ton are intimately familiar. I am speaking, of course, of the Duchess of Ravensgrave, formerly Helena Darrow.

She sucked in a sharp breath of air. The writer had lacked even the usual decency merely to allude to his subject. With growing horror, she searched the rest of the first page. There was her name again. Distantly, she knew it would be best to cast the pamphlet aside and read no further. Doing so would only serve to upset her, but she found herself unable to resist.

One would imagine that plaguing Lord Greene so harshly that this noble man took his own life would be enough to satisfy the wretched woman, but it was not. This writer has learned that she has taken her sins up north and now wreaks havoc in Yorkshire, plotting to destroy another well-bred and foolish man.

Helena inhaled deeply, clutching the papers so tightly that they nearly tore in her hands. Her first, instinctive thought was that the pamphlet must be Sir Bertram's design, for its timing—just after the Greythorne Assembly—could not possibly be coincidental. However, Helena had so many enemies that she could not be certain. It was equally plausible that the pamphlet had come from one of Lord Greene's aggrieved relatives, or some slanderer who sought to make a small sum from maligning her once more, now that her name would be again of note.

"You look distressed."

Meg's voice shook Helena from her thoughts. The older woman stood by the door, brow creased with concern.

"It is nothing," Helena said. "Just—just some slander."

But it did not really matter if the pamphlet was slanderous. If people believed its contents, that was nearly as bad as if it had been true.

"Slander?" Meg asked. "Against you?"

Helena wordlessly held out the pamphlet. Meg took it and opened it. After a heartbeat, a sharp gasp tore from the woman's throat.

"I know," Helena said. "It is... dreadful. Lucien and I must decide how to answer these accusations."

"You do not think he will believe this," Meg said, her eyes wide.

Helena forced down the lump that rose in her throat. She twisted her hands in her skirts. "Of course not."

But he might. Even if they were something almost like friends, she could not count on him to believe her, much less continue to stand by her when his own reputation risked being ruined. What if he sent her away? Or worse, what if he chose to annul the marriage? He might claim that he had not known all these terrible things about her.

Helena's pulse quickened. Her mouth strained into a forced smile, for Meg's benefit as much as her own. If she let herself follow those treacherous thoughts, Helena thought she might very well begin crying. "I am going to breakfast," she said. "Please, do not tell Edmund. There is no reason for him to worry."

"Of course," Meg said, crushing the pamphlet in her hand.

Helena went to the dining room, her spirits sinking a little when she found only Beatrice and Edmund there. "Where is Lucien?" Helena asked as she took her usual seat. "And Lady Honora?"

Beatrice smiled wryly. "I thought to ask you the same thing."

Tea and honey cakes were brought. Helena's eyes darted to the staff who carried them, searching for any sign that they might have seen the pamphlet and read its contents. That was absurd, of course. Word would not have spread so quickly through the household, would it?

Neither Beatrice nor Edmund seemed aware of the pamphlet and its contents. Helena bit the inside of her cheek. Not only had someone written that accursed thing, but someone had also sent it to her. Someone had wanted her to see it. Doubtless, the aim had been to upset her. Such an aim had succeeded, for Helena knew there must be other pamphlets. How many? How far had they spread, and who had possession of them?

"You are quiet this morning," Beatrice said. "Is something amiss?"

Edmund's eyes widened. Helena forced a smile, aware of her brother's stare on her. She had let Edmund believe that everything was well, that all the scandals and fears were behind them, and she could not bear to have her words proven false by some cruel slanderer.

"Nothing," Helena said. "I am merely a little tired. The Greythorne Assembly was a little more strenuous than I had anticipated."

"Did it go well?" Edmund asked. "I know it was rather important."

"Well enough," Helena said.

Certainly, it could have gone worse. Having found the pamphlet, she wondered if the Greythorne Assembly had been quite the success she had thought, though.

"That is good," Beatrice said. "I told Aunt Honora that you and Lucien would be fine. She was dreadfully worried about you both."

"For good reason!" Lady Honora's voice filled the room, pitched louder than usual.

Helena's heart sank, for she recognized the pamphlet in Lady Honora's hand even before she sat and laid it beside her cup of tea.

"You had best prepare yourself, Helena," Lady Honora said. "The village is humming with word of what you have done."

"It is untrue," Helena replied, her heart hammering against her ribcage. "That pamphlet lies about me. It tries to paint me as a monster that I am not and never have been."

Lady Honora took her cup of tea and slowly raised it to her lips. "Truth is irrelevant. People will believe what they wish to believe, and the more tantalising a rumour, the more eager they are to believe it."

The honey cake tasted like ash in Helena's mouth. It was only logical that she and Lady Honora ought to be allies in this situation, for they both only wanted what was best for Lucien and the dukedom, but Helena could not shake the prickling unease that Lady Honora might be pleased with this turn of events.

"Do you know where Lucien is?" Helena asked.

"Away," Lady Honora said.

"What is the matter?" Beatrice asked, leaning across the table to see the pamphlet.

With a scowl, Lady Honora handed the pamphlet to her niece. "Another scandal that this house does not need! I told him this would happen."

Helena silently wished that the ground would swallow her whole.

"What is it?" Edmund asked.

"Nothing I cannot deal with," Helena said, gathering her courage. "As Lady Honora said, I must be prepared, and I will be."

***

Although Helena had mustered up a little bravery when seated at the breakfast table, she found her determination waning as the day brought even more pamphlets. Whoever had sent the first had no wish to relent. Meg had found one tucked into the side gate. Edmund had spied boys from the village carrying them.

With every whispered word of a pamphlet, ice crept more insistently in Helena's veins. Ravensgrave began to feel like a cage, her own refuge from the monstrous sheets and vicious rumours circling just outside the estate. She had retired early, unable to find the appetite to eat dinner, and had lain awake throughout the night. Helena found that she was strangely numb to everything, as if she were simultaneously thinking too deeply about the pamphlets and not deeply enough.

At last, restlessness began to take hold. Just before dawn, she rose and dressed. The house was as silent as a tomb and just as still. Helena slipped into the gardens, her breath frosting the air. A chill suffused the morning, sinking all the way down into her bones. She entered the conservatory, just barely touched by the light of day.

Helena worked for a long time, trimming back the ivy and replanting the crushed hyssop. It was easy, methodical work that did not entirely keep her mind away from the pamphlet, but the familiar motions, at least, meant she was doing something. If only life could be remedied as easily as a broken plant!

The door creaked open behind her. Helena saw the face reflected in the glass wall of the conservatory. "Lucien."

She scarcely dared to breathe, for fear that he might vanish like the morning's dew. Helena had not seen him in an entire day. He walked quietly to her, his boots crunching the stone beneath them.

Did he know about the pamphlets? He must, certainly, or he would not have left. Helena's chest tightened. Perhaps Lucien had needed some time to decide what ought to be done with her. Maybe he had found his answer. He crouched beside her, saying nothing. For a heartbeat, the entire world seemed to hold its breath. Helena swallowed, trying to find the words she wanted most to ask: *Do you know, and what are you going to do?*

She was so seldom hesitant, but she found that the thought of his answer filled her with a deep-seated knot of terror. He gingerly brushed a small clump of dirt from her hand, and something in Helena broke. His hand drifted further up her arm, and she turned, burying herself in his embrace. She pressed her face into his shoulder, inhaling the scent of Bay Rum and the earth.

"Oh, Helena," he sighed.

He pulled her into his lap and wrapped his arms around her. Helena's eyes burned, and she forced back the threatening tears. She dug her fingers into the lapels of his coat, as if by holding on to him she might keep herself together.

"I thought you might send me away," she said, her throat thick and her words shaking. "It would be easier for you if I were gone."

Lucien held her more tightly. "I will not. Not ever."

She sobbed against his shoulder, shaking as he rubbed gentle circles on her back. "Please..."

"Anything, Helena," he said. "What do you need from me?"

"Make it better."

She could not have quite said what she meant. Perhaps she had no particular thing in mind when she made her desperate, broken request. Lucien seized a handful of her skirts, slowly hitching them up her thighs. "Perhaps a distraction," he murmured.

She nodded, the rough wool of his coat rubbing against her cheek. Lucien's gloved hand slipped between her warm thighs, and her whole body shivered in anticipation. A distraction, indeed.

He traced a quick path to her core, gently rubbing Helena's sensitive nub. She curled her fingers more tightly in his coat, her breath hitching unevenly.

Lucien tilted his head, his lips brushing her cheek. His breath was warm and steadying, despite the coldness of the world around them. "I will make you feel so very good, Helena," he murmured.

"Please," she whispered.

She bucked her hips as he circled her core. Helena's thighs trembled, and sweat gathered at the small of her back. She pressed her face to the side of his neck, aware of the warm tears that finally slipped free against her wishes. He drew his finger between her folds, tracing with agonising slowness. Her body shook, her muscles tightening with the promise of pleasure yet to come.

He pressed one finger inside her, and Helena's back arched. A gasp tore from her throat as her inner walls clenched around him. Lucien worked her quickly, every motion firm but never rough. Helena quivered as the familiar wave of pleasure crashed through her. Black spots obscured her vision, and she clung to him, letting her body relax in the warmth that followed her release.

Lucien kissed her hair. "Better?" he murmured.

"Just a little."

He kissed her again and held her, the only sound their breaths mingling together in the air, and Helena thought that she—just might—manage to keep herself together.

Chapter Twenty-Two

At last, Helena drew back—just enough to gaze at him with a soft expression. Lucien's pulse jumped. His body ached for her, his hand tingling with the phantom touch of his finger inside her sex. "Shall we continue?" he asked.

"Here?" she whispered.

He laughed, his eyes sweeping over the hard stone and the plants, many of them only recently restored to health through Helena's efforts. "Not necessarily. It looks rather uncomfortable."

Her lips twitched into a small smile. "Perhaps, in the house."

"Perhaps."

Lucien hefted her into his arms and held her close, drawing a cry of surprise from her. He carried her from the conservatory. Helena's body still trembled, and in the early dawn, he spied the trails left by tears upon her cheeks. She smelled of the ground and morning air, mingled with sweat from her labours. Everything inside Lucien softened. In his arms, she seemed somehow more fragile than she ever had been. He ached to draw her close and protect her from everything that he had drawn her into—from all the stares and whispers and pamphlets. From all the judgment.

They entered the hall without anyone seeing them. As he reached the base of the stairs, Helena's hand curled in his shirt. "Yes?" he murmured.

She gazed at him with beseeching eyes. "I do not want to go to my room."

He did not ask why. Instead, he merely nodded and went to his own chambers. His bedchamber was bathed in the soft light of the sun, all the shadows dulled. Lucien placed Helena gingerly at the edge of his bed. She reluctantly released her hold on him. He knelt before her and searched for her ankle beneath the folds of her skirts. Lucien carefully removed her half-damp boots, one after the other, and set them neatly aside.

"You know about the pamphlets," she said softly.

How could he not?

"I do," he said.

He caressed her ankles, delicate and warm in his hands. "They remain outside of Ravensgrave. I will see to that. You are safe here."

He offered a hand and aided Helena to her feet. She stood before him, silent and warm. And perhaps, wanting.

"Undress." His words were more a question than an order, as soft as he could make them.

Her breath hitched as she removed her pelisse. Helena's fingers trembled as she undid the buttons. Lucien considered asking if she might like aid, but he decided that it was best to wait. He wanted Helena to decide if she wanted this; he could not influence her decision. After she removed the pelisse, she held it to him like an offering.

Lucien smiled and draped it over the nearby chair. Then he lowered himself into it, watching. A pink flush spread across Helena's face.

"If you have changed your mind, we do not have to continue with this," he said gently. "We can return to our rooms and pretend that nothing happened."

"I know."

She slowly removed her dress, and Lucien's blood roared in his ears. Helena appeared to be an angel, clad all in white, with the sunlight settled in her hair so that it appeared like a halo about her head. Lucien's gaze fell to her breasts, so white and soft, as Helena deftly undid her stays. His throat went dry as she pulled them away and cast them aside.

Lucien's loins stirred. Helena removed her chemise, unveiling her perfect body to his eyes. She was soft and curvaceous, like a statue of Aphrodite, and when she stood before him—her eyes wide and her hands twitching, as though with the urge to cover herself—Lucien let out a low, longing sigh. "You are so perfect," he murmured.

"You exaggerate," she huffed.

But Helena's eyes betrayed her mirth and, beneath that, something that might have been gratitude.

Lucien removed his boots and stockings. His coat came next, his body aching as he tried to affect the same unhurried pace that she had. He managed it until he tossed the coat onto the floor and heard a pleasant hitch of Helena's breath. Then his composure fell to pieces. He tore his jacket and waistcoat off, followed by his shirt. His trousers stretched so tightly around his manhood that they hurt, and when he unfastened them, his length sprang forth, already hard and eager for the warmth of Helena's cunny.

She slowly reached for him, and Lucien gathered the tattered remnants of his restraint. Helena had survived another terrible ordeal, for the slander must weigh heavily upon her mind. She needed his patience and gentleness. His kindness.

He would make this slow and gentle for her. Lucien inhaled, steadying himself, and caught her wrist, placing a gentle kiss upon her knuckles. "Are you certain, Helena?" he murmured. "We do not have to do anything that displeases you."

Helena nodded, her lips pursed together in determination. Lucien tilted his head and kissed her. It was a slow and lingering kiss, like a butterfly lighting upon a flower. He drew her into his arms, leisurely pulling the pins from her hair and letting them fall to the floor with faint, metallic sounds.

She wrapped her arms around his neck and tentatively returned his kisses. Lucien pressed his lips into the crook of her neck, down to her shoulder, and to her collarbone. With every kiss, he inhaled the sweetness of English lavender and rose oil, accompanied by the faint sharpness of her earlier release.

"Shall we try the bed now?" he murmured against her clavicle.

Helena shifted back and moved onto the bed. Lucien gazed at her, admiring the full length of her nude body spread over the bed linens. Her chest rose and fell quickly, and the flush from her face had spread downwards to her chest. He brought himself onto the bed, straddling her waist. "Leave everything to me," he murmured into her ear.

His manhood twitched, the ache between his thighs so insistent that it bordered on painful. It took all his strength of will to trail kisses slowly from her jaw downward. He kissed her throat, her shoulder, her breasts, and her stomach. She shivered and stirred beneath him, soft groans tearing from between her coral lips. Helena's fingers curled in his hair, drawing his head down to her. Lucien cupped her breasts in his hands and coaxed her nipples into hard, sensitive peaks.

"Lucien," she whispered, her voice nearly reverent. "Oh, please..."

"I will," he murmured, kissing the valley between her breasts. "I promise."

Her thighs pressed against his sides, her core hot and damp against his stomach. Lucien traced his hands over her ribs and kissed her stomach. Helena's breath quickened, her body jolting. She lowered her hands to the bed linens, taking great fistfuls of the fabric between her slender fingers. "Lucien," she murmured.

He shifted further down the bed and held her hips, gently tracing her hip bones. The tight curls around her sex brushed against the tip of his manhood. Lucien looked at her, her eyes wide with wonder and her lips slightly parted.

"Shall I?" he asked. "I shall be so very careful."

Helena nodded. Lucien pressed his thumb against her nub, and her hips bucked. She unleashed a high-pitched, feminine cry as he traced slow and gentle circles before dipping his finger between her folds. Helena was already wet, but still he took his time. He stretched her carefully with his thumb before gingerly adding another finger. Helena groaned raggedly, her body jolting up towards him. She brushed against the length of his manhood, and Lucien groaned, nearly undone by the sudden movement.

"Be careful, Helena," he said throatily.

She laughed, the sound nearly breathless.

Lucien took his manhood in hand and lined himself up to her entrance. Helena's fingers twisted the bed linens more tightly. Slowly, he lowered himself into her, coaxing her body to open to his girth. Helena inhaled deeply, and he watched her face for any sign of discomfort. Their eyes met, and she offered a small, tentative smile. "Please, continue. I cannot bear waiting much longer."

He pressed his manhood inside her. Helena gasped, shifting her hips. Lucien hissed between his teeth, for she was quite tight. He grasped her hips, firmly but not unkindly. "Relax," he murmured. "I will wait until you are ready."

Her breaths came in loud, uneven gasps for air. She slowly, hesitantly rocked against him. Lucien tossed his head back with a hiss; his thighs quivered with his efforts not to find release. Did Helena even realise how alluring she was? Did she have any inkling of how badly his body ached for hers?

Slowly, she found her rhythm, moving her hips so his manhood pushed more gently inside her. Helena's face reddened with exertion from her labours, and a low whine tore from between her lips.

"Lucien!" she cried. "Oh!"

"Are you ready?" he asked kindly.

She looked in need of great gentleness. In his bed, Helena seemed somehow transformed into someone else, someone soft and vulnerable and without all the fire he often associated with her. The pamphlets must have weighed terribly on her. Lucien clenched his jaw. How could someone—likely Sir Bertram—hurt Helena like that? How could any man live with himself, knowing that he had brought this brazen and confident woman to tears and seeking comfort?

And Lucien wanted very much to give her comfort and affection and whatever else she might desire, but that did not change the truth that someone had hurt Helena, wounded her so deeply.

"Yes," she breathed. "I am ready now."

Lucien rocked his hips steadily, his loins tightening and his release growing with every movement. She met his thrusts with bucks of her hips and wordless cries. When Lucien increased his pace, she gasped. Helena threw her head back against the bed linens, every movement jolting her body. Her thighs quivered, and his muscles strained.

He clenched his jaw, determined to withhold his own satisfaction until she found hers, but it was so very hard. His whole body burned for release, his muscles twitching and straining with the effort. Helena gasped and clutched wildly at the bed linens. "Oh, yes!" she cried.

They shook together, and as Helena's inner walls clenched about his length, her release tearing through her shuddering body, Lucien allowed his own restraint to snap. He gasped from the force of his release. Pleasure swept over him, so intense that his vision went white for just an instant. He spilled his hot seed into Helena. A low groan tore from her throat, and she gazed at him with something like wonder.

Lucien withdrew gently and lay on his side beside her. Helena's lips remained slightly parted as she drank in greedy gulps of air. He smiled and reached out, hesitantly.

"What is it?" She sounded raw and harried, urgent even.

Lucien slowly brushed his knuckles over her cheekbone. She inhaled softly and leaned into his touch. He gingerly, slowly tucked a wayward lock of hair behind her ear.

"I love you."

He blinked, uncertain that he had heard the confession.

Helena's eyes widened, and she audibly gulped. "I—I—"

His heart hammered against his ribs. "Say it again."

Lucien must have misheard her, or perhaps he had misunderstood her tone. Maybe Helena had said it in jest. His heart clenched at the thought, for he did not want to think that he might be mistaken or that she might be teasing him.

"I love you," she whispered, as if she were making some private confession.

"And I love you." He spoke without hesitation, without a second thought.

Inside, Lucien was a maelstrom of feelings that he could not even put to name, but he knew that the words were true. Truer than any he had ever spoken.

Helena closed her eyes, her face softening, and he pulled the bed linens over them. Lucien drew her close, so her soft body was tucked against his. They would have to face the slanderer and the pamphlets very soon, but for just a moment, he and Helena were safe from the world.

Chapter Twenty-Three

Days passed, and the pamphlets grew. It seemed to Helena as if they sprang from the air itself, appearing without warning in the strangest places—the gates outside, in the library, the ballroom, the kitchens. Meg rose each morning and gathered them up, tossing them in the fireplace before the staff could read them. At first, it had seemed a good idea, even clever, but as days turned to weeks, the futility of it began to sink in. The staff knew. No one in Ravensgrave could possibly have missed what was happening.

It was as though the pamphlets had taken a life of their own—like a persistent gentleman at a ball who refused to be dissuaded from dancing with a lady who detested him, a gentleman who looked rather like Sir Bertram. As Helena sat at dinner, her eyes fixed listlessly upon the roasted pheasant on her plate, she found her fingers drifting towards Lucien's hand without any conscious thought.

"Meg seems tired." Edmund's voice was quiet, wavering a little.

"We are all tired," Lady Honora said stiffly. "It is proper not to show fatigue."

Edmund seemed to wilt a little in his chair, even as his face reddened in what Helena suspected was offence on Meg's behalf.

"Well," Beatrice said brightly, "it is not as though we can be harassed with the pamphlets forever. The printer would not have a limitless number of copies."

"It seems as if they do," Edmund muttered, stabbing the pheasant with his fork, as if it might be to blame for all their woes.

196

Helena realised that her jaw was clenched tightly, and she slowly loosened it, forcing herself to breathe.

"We must appear unconcerned with the matter," Lady Honora said, still stiff. "Acting as if we are concerned with the contents will be perceived as a sign of guilt."

"As will not reacting," Lucien countered. "It seems as though there is no correct course of action."

Lady Honora smiled thinly and said nothing. Helena could sense what the woman wished to say: *This is your fault for marrying Helena.*

"Do we have any sense of how far the pamphlets might have spread?" Helena asked. "And who might be lending credence to them? Certainly, there must be some in the ton who do not believe those lies."

"One would think," Lucien said. "We cannot count on such people for allies, though. Even those who believe you to be innocent will be hesitant to become embroiled in a scandal without some clear benefit in doing so."

"And I doubt you can offer any," Lady Honora said, stiff as ever. "All the progress you might have made at the Greythorne Assembly will be undone by this pamphlet!"

Edmund gasped abruptly, jolting to his feet. He had accidentally toppled a goblet, spilling lemonade over the table. Helena straightened the goblet, silently searching for something with which to clean the mess. One of the staff swept in to do so. Helena watched silently, only belatedly remembering that she was a duchess, and duchesses did not clean.

Lucien said nothing. He continued eating, as though he had not even noticed anything.

"I am sorry," Edmund said, his lower lip quivering.

"There is no reason to apologise," Lucien murmured. "I think I will retire."

"As will we," Lady Honora said, jerking her chin towards Beatrice. "It has been a trying day."

Beatrice wrinkled her nose, seeming displeased. Her sharp eyes darted to Helena's face, her expression softening with sympathy. The women left the room, and Lucien slowly rose. He pressed his palms flat against the table and lowered his head. A deep sigh tore from him. "Good evening, wife."

She nodded, unable to find the words or will to return his remark. He strode behind her chair, as if they were strangers. Helena clasped her hands in her lap and closed her eyes, aching for the closeness he had shown in his bedroom just a few short weeks ago.

Helena and Edmund were left alone. Her brother pushed back his chair and stood, walking to the window. Outside, the twilight gathered. "Is it true that everyone hates us?" Edmund asked, his voice quivering.

Yes.

Helena forced a smile and shook her head. "No, of course not."

She joined him by the window and pulled Edmund into a tight hug, her breath hitching. Helena had tried so very hard to shield him from it all, and when faced with her failure, her chest ached. She would have given anything to undo it, to repair all the damage she had inadvertently caused, but she could not.

Something had to change, though. Helena pressed her lips into a thin line, thinking. She had not left Ravensgrave in weeks, hoping to stay safe inside the crumbling estate, but she knew one thing: the sender of the pamphlets was either lingering nearby or else had an accomplice in the house.

She must find Sir Bertram—or whoever he had sent in his stead—and she must confront that person. Even if Helena could not stop the endless litany of pamphlets, it was not as if she could make the situation worse. Doing anything was better than nothing at all.

***

The next morning, Helena's choice was made. She dressed plainly, choosing to forgo her usual gloves and ribbons. "Are you going to breakfast?" Meg asked.

"No," Helena said. "I have business outside of Ravensgrave today."

Before Meg could question her further, Helena left the room with the intent of going to the village. She spied Edmund lingering by the stairs and smiled wanly. "Enjoy your morning," she said, hoping that her voice did not quiver. "I will return before supper."

Helena went to the stables, waving away the stableboys who hastened to aid her, and mounted a white mare whose name was Aurora. Soon, she set out along the familiar path and down to the village. Her heart hammered against her ribs. She had no notion of how she might find Sir Bertram or his accomplice, but the village was not large. Someone would know where the pamphlets came from, and she had only to ask.

As she rode into the village, the villagers cast her sharp looks before hurrying away with whispers and laughs poorly concealed behind hands. Helena's blood roared in her ears. She thought she had prepared herself for this encounter, that she would not be wounded by the villagers' distaste, but with every glance and smirk, ice sank into her veins.

199

"Your Grace."

She halted abruptly, stifling a gasp. Helena's head snapped in the direction of the voice, certain that in her fatigue she must have imagined the sound that came from the nearest alley. Then Sir Bertram stepped forward. He bowed mockingly. "Helena."

Her jaw clenched, and her hands tightened on her horse's reins. "I would have thought you would have something better to do than linger about the village and torment me."

He smiled thinly. The man stood across the street, just before the assembly house. Helena considered dismounting, but she felt—instinctively—as though she ought to keep some distance from him. She did not know what he might do in the open street, where anyone might see them, but she did not wish to learn.

"Have I been tormenting you?" he asked. "Such cruel words for an old friend."

"You presume too much," Helena argued. "We have never been—and never will be—friends."

Sir Bertram shook his head in mock dismay. "Such harsh words do not suit any lady, much less a duchess."

She clenched her jaw. "What must I do to make you stop with the pamphlets?"

He laughed. "Why, nothing!"

"Nothing?" she asked. "What do you want from me? An apology? To see me humiliated?"

"Oh." His expression became coy. "You still believe the pamphlets are about you. I regret to inform you that you are not the centre of my world, Helena. You were never the target of my attacks. It was always Ashmore that I was attacking. You were merely convenient bait."

She inhaled sharply. "What?"

"There is to be a final assembly before the London Season begins, where we will forge alliances for the coming Season. Since the Greythorne Assembly did not happen as I wished, I was forced to resort to… other means of gaining votes. I never cared about besmirching your virtue, but doing so was convenient."

A lump lodged in Helena's throat. "You are foul," she rasped.

"Politics," he said, shrugging. "I would not expect you to understand that."

"You will not succeed," Helena said. "Lucien is too clever to be thwarted by someone like you."

"So you say," Sir Bertram answered, "but you do not know how far those pamphlets have spread through the countryside and beyond."

Helena inhaled sharply and turned away with her horse. She coaxed the animal into a trot, her pulse jumping as she rode back to Ravensgrave. Sir Bertram himself had come to the village and potentially spent a very long time there. He did not merely wish to best Lucien. Helena feared that the man wished to ruin him entirely.

***

Bertram nodded to the two men he had waiting across the street. They would follow Helena discreetly back to Ravensgrave. His lips curved as he watched her retreat. Bertram had fully anticipated that someone at Ravensgrave would eventually seek him out in the village. It did not take a brilliant mind to realise that he might be lurking nearby, given how numerous the pamphlets were.

He had thought it would be Ashmore, and that the man might do something foolish in an attempt to preserve Helena's honour. Bertram had already written the encounter in his mind, poised to paint the most unflattering portrait of Ashmore that he could. After all, the man would have no proof that Bertram was the secret author of the pamphlets.

Helena's arrival changed everything, though. "Well," Bertram said, smirking. "I think the ton would have much to say about a scandalous, married woman choosing to have a secret meeting with a former suitor."

He turned away, deciding how he might craft the narrative to absolve himself of blame for the encounter. Bertram would insist that he was the innocent victim. Perhaps he might suggest that Helena deceived him into coming to the village.

Yes, of course. Bertram's fingers twitched, exhilaration rushing through him. While harming Helena was not his aim, there was a sort of satisfaction in vexing the woman who had dared to choose someone else. He would write that she had invited him to the village, insisting that he and Ashmore meet in secret to resolve their differences. When Bertram arrived, it was only she who greeted him.

As he neared the small inn where he was staying, he grinned. It would be the perfect story to ruin both Lucien and Helena. By the time the Mayleigh Assembly met, Lucien's reputation would be in tatters. He would have no means of finding support. Indeed, the man might not even care to be in London when the Season came!

"Oh, Helena," Bertram said mockingly. "You proved to be useful, after all."

Now he had only to write quickly, so he could have that manuscript on Finch's desk. Then it would be spread throughout the countryside, just as the pamphlet had been. If Helena had found *The Ashmore Marriage* troublesome, she had no inkling of the storm that awaited her.

Chapter Twenty-Four

Aunt Honora whirled around when Lucien entered the study. "Have you seen this?" she asked.

Lucien sighed and ran a hand through his hair. The pamphlets had ceased two weeks earlier, and he had thought that they might all finally have some reprieve. However, the manner in which Aunt Honora held the page in her hand suggested that he had been too optimistic. There seemed to be some new torment on the horizon.

"What is it?" Lucien asked, wearily sinking into the nearby chair.

"A scandal sheet," his aunt replied stiffly. "You might recognise the name."

She held out the offending sheet, and he hissed between his teeth: *Helena Ashmore, Duchess of Ravensgrave, was seen in the company of a gentleman, who is quite familiar with the ton and to her.*

"Shall I read it to you?" Aunt Honora's lips curled. "It is quite a titillating tale. It alleges that your wife met Sir Bertram alone and that several witnesses observed the intimacy between them."

"I do not believe it," Lucien said, his voice rough. "Helena would never show any intimacy to that man."

Aunt Honora cast him a stern look. "According to this sheet, Sir Bertram was lured into the village under false pretences. Helena invited him to meet in the village—a quiet place that would remain unnoticed—so that the three of you could set aside your differences and make amends."

"No one would believe that!" he scoffed. "If I wished to meet with Sir Bertram, I would do it at Ravensgrave."

"You are right," Aunt Honora said. "People will observe that it is strange, but that does not mean they will not believe the claims. The *ton* enjoys a scandal, and they will only be too eager to believe this one."

He swore softly and chose to ignore Aunt Honora's reproachful look. "I must prove that none of it is true," Lucien said. "I will speak to Helena, and—"

"And are you certain that she did not meet with him?"

"I already said that she did not!"

"No," Aunt Honora said. "You said that you did not believe she would show intimacy towards Sir Bertram. That does not mean she did not meet with him, and if she did... if there are witnesses—"

"There will not be!" he snapped, swiping the scandal sheet from her grasp. "I will confront Helena, and she will tell me that there is nothing amiss!"

His aunt stiffened. "I hope you are right, because that scandal sheet paints you as a cuckold. *The duke, it seems, was not enough to satisfy her ambitions or her appetite,*" she said, with the cadence of someone who had read the words often. "You must set it right at once."

Sheet clasped in his hand, Lucien stalked from the room. He knew precisely where Helena would be—the conservatory, which was looking nearly restored on the inside. Lucien clenched his jaw as he crossed the gardens and entered through the battered door. He would need to fix the outside, so it was worthier of what Helena had done to the interior.

But another time. As he approached her, he was not seized by hot fury. Instead, it was as though he had fallen into an icy lake. It was difficult to think and breathe clearly, especially when she turned to him, distracted from her task of pruning the roses. Helena looked beautiful, surrounded by the greenery as she was; her lips slightly parted, the sign of a question yet to be asked.

"Is it true?" he asked before she could.

"Is what true?"

"Did you meet Sir Bertram in the village?"

Helena paused, her eyes darting to the page in his hand. Lucien fought the urge to rip it to pieces then and there. That heartbeat of silence had told him as much as any verbal confirmation could have.

"How could you?" he asked. "What were you thinking?"

"I met with him," she said. "Alone. It was only once, and I— I knew that either he or one of his associates had to be nearby. Someone was leaving the pamphlets. You suspected him, too."

"Yes, but I did not—that does not explain why you went to meet with him!" Lucien snapped. "Do you have any idea what damage you have caused? Your little encounter is in the scandal sheets, and it sounds far more scandalous than what I imagine actually occurred!"

All the colour drained from her face. "What does it say?"

"It claims that I am insufficient for fulfilling your needs," he said. "Not that it matters what it says. What were you thinking in meeting him like that?"

"I wanted to protect us!" she exclaimed. "To protect my family! I thought you would want that, too."

He stared at her, something inside him threatening to bubble up and burst. "I am your family, too!" Lucien exclaimed. "I am your husband! Or have you forgotten that?"

She flinched. "Of course I have not forgotten that."

"But you did not trust me! You could have come to me and asked me to accompany you," Lucien said. "You could have made the suggestion to me, and I would have listened."

Helena's brow furrowed. Her eyes sparked with familiar fire and defiance, but there was something strangely vulnerable in her face. She was trapped, he realised. Helena had no answer—or perhaps no answer that would be persuasive.

"Get out of my conservatory," he said. "I—I need to think."

She tipped her chin up. "If I had told you my plan, you would not have allowed it."

"I suppose we will never know, will we?"

Helena nodded stiffly. As she walked past him, his restraint snapped, and he tore the scandal sheet in half.

"Lucien," she said.

He did not turn to face her. "I want to be alone."

"I know," Helena said. "But you should know that I was not Sir Bertram's target. You were. I fear he seeks to ruin you."

"He will fail."

He anticipated argument, but none came. Lucien stood there a while longer. After some time, he looked over his shoulder, half-expecting Helena to be standing behind him still.

But she was not.

***

That night, Helena did not sleep. After a few hours of staring silently at the dark ceiling and trying to find rest, she decided that none was coming. Peace seemed equally out of reach.

I do not belong here.

Her chest ached, and tears threatened her eyes. The conversation with Lucien kept playing in her mind, as if she were watching it all performed on a stage again and again. She had not trusted him. That was not because she did not trust him; it had been only a moment of weakness, a single instant when she had thought it best not to involve him. Worse, she had not even really regretted that choice. She had only regretted the encounter with Sir Bertram after being caught.

Helena had been used against Lucien the first time, but the second time had been her own doing. Her breath hitched, and she clenched the bed linens as if her life depended on them. For some time, she was alone with her thoughts.

Still, she rose before dawn and crept to Edmund's room. He slept peacefully, his pale face softened with sleep and traced in moonlight. Helena's chest ached. For a heartbeat, she considered returning to her room, packing, and leaving. Lucien had more means to care for her brother than she did.

"Helena?" he mumbled, blinking blearily at her.

It was not too late for her to insist that she had just come to see how he was. It was not too late for her to leave alone. Helena sighed. Maybe this was a selfish choice, but there was no one in all the world whom she loved as much as her brother. She could not leave him.

"We are leaving," she said softly. "I need to pack and write some letters. Gather what you need and be ready."

He nodded, eyes wide. Helena embraced him once and kissed the top of his head. Then she made haste back to her bedchamber. Her eyes fell upon everything she owned, a startling amount of it accumulated during her short time as the Duchess of Ravensgrave. Helena's chest ached. She would take only the necessary things.

Helena gathered her two favourite dresses, carefully folding them into her satchel, and her manuscript. There were a few coins, which Helena had kept in her reticule in case Lucien had turned out to be the monster that she had feared. She almost wished he had been. Then leaving would have been simple.

Once everything was gathered, she went to her writing desk and withdrew two sheets of paper from one of the drawers. Helena took a deep breath and dipped the waiting pen in ink.

Dearest Husband—

Helena paused. Her chest and throat were both tight, and her heart beat so loudly and quickly that she felt like a rabbit caught in a snare. Did she truly have to go? It was not too late to undo the decision, to tell Edmund that she had changed her mind, and slip into her bed once again. Helena's whole body slumped, as if a great weight held her down and sought to bury her. The damage was done. Could her presence even worsen the situation when it was already so dire?

She inhaled softly. If nothing else, she was a distraction. At worst, Lucien would grow to resent her.

I want to apologise for all the difficulties that I have caused you, she wrote. *It was never my intention to cause you such grievous harm, yet the damage is done. You are right; I should have trusted you.*

Helena paused and bit the inside of her cheek, her mind racing for words that might accurately reflect the depth of the emotions swirling about inside her, but all words seemed inadequate and limited in their expression.

Haltingly, she pressed the pen once more to paper.

In all honesty, I think that I should not have come to Ravensgrave at all. We would both be better for it. I refuse to be your burden any longer, and I hope that my absence may help you recover your reputation, if only in some small measure. I know that the situation may seem bleak now, but eventually the shadows will lift. When they do, I hope you find a wife who is worthy of you.

Forever yours,

Helena

She folded the letter and scrawled his name across it. Helena did not imagine that it would take long for the letter to be discovered. She pressed her fingers along the crease of the fold, as if she were making a promise with how she touched the page.

There was only one matter left to resolve. Helena's hands trembled as she touched the remaining sheet of paper and pressed the tip of her pen to it.

Dear Meg—

If Helena asked Meg to flee with her, she had no doubts that the woman would. Meg had followed her all over Britain, through both the good and the bad, but of late, Meg had been...

So very tired.

You have cared for Edmund and me for so very long, Helena wrote. *You deserve better than having to always chase after me. I wish you all the best and hope that you might find the happiness you deserve.*

I have left a letter for Lucien. Please, do not tell him that I have gone. He will discover that soon enough on his own.

Helena blinked back tears as she read the words again. They did not seem to express all that she felt for Meg—all that she had been to Edmund and herself—but Helena doubted she could ever express that.

A tear rolled down her cheek, and Helena quickly wiped it away before it could stain the page. Her breath came in a great, heaving gasp for air as she signed her name and left the letter.

Taking her satchel, she slipped quietly from the room. She met Edmund in his bedchamber, his own sparse possessions in a bag of their own and slung over his right shoulder.

"We have to go," she said softly, offering her hand.

"We cannot even bid everyone farewell?" he asked, his voice quivering just a little.

"No," Helena said. "Or they will not let us leave."

Edmund nodded and placed his hand in hers. "I just wish we did not have to leave."

"I know," Helena said. "But I—I promise that it is for the best. Everything will be better for them if we are gone, and we will find somewhere that we can be happy together. Just the two of us."

Edmund's expression became determined, and Helena's heart ached. Even if this was the right decision, committing to it felt like surrendering a part of herself that she might never see returned to her.

Chapter Twenty-Five

When Helena did not join him for breakfast, Lucien assumed that she was avoiding him. He supposed she had gone to the conservatory or, perhaps, had decided to spend some time with Edmund. As the hours ticked by, however, an inkling that something was amiss began to curl in the pit of his stomach. Edmund had not yet made an appearance either.

He had spied Meg going about her usual duties in the morning, and the woman had appeared unusually pale to him. Lucien had thought it might simply be the strain of the pamphlets and scandal sheets that had taken control of Meg, but he was slowly becoming less certain.

"Where are you?" Lucien muttered, standing at the entrance of his study. He drummed his fingers upon the open doorway, his eyes sweeping over the shelves.

The library was one of Helena's preferred haunts, and he had somewhat anticipated that she might be curled behind the shelves, lost in some volume—or perhaps sulking. However, she was not.

He walked into the foyer next, hurrying to the gardens. Lucien cast his gaze wide, searching for her familiar shape. When he did not find her, he walked briskly to the conservatory. "Helena?" he called.

Lucien received no answer. Pulse quickening, he returned the way he had come and entered the house once more. Cold dread shot through him. She had not—

He scarcely dared to complete the terrible thought. Helena could not be gone. It must be mere unfortunate circumstance that he had seen neither her nor Edmund that day. The pale complexion of Helena's maid, Meg, was also most assuredly just a coincidence.

There was no significance in any of it beyond unfortunate timing. Still, Lucien's thoughts refused to believe that nothing was amiss. They spiralled inside him, like a hive of disturbed bees, becoming increasingly dreadful with every passing beat of his heart.

"Oh!"

Lucien was so consumed by his thoughts that he nearly crashed into Beatrice. Her cry of surprise still rang in his ears.

"Helena!" he said brusquely. "Have you seen her?"

Beatrice blinked at him, visibly taken aback. "No. Has something happened?"

"Nothing," he said. "Nothing—but I must—I must find her at once!"

Lucien darted up the stairs towards Helena's room, taking them two at a time in his haste to find her. Perhaps the distress caused by the pamphlets and the scandal sheets had made her develop a headache or similar ailment. Maybe Edmund had chosen to provide his sister with company, and that was why he had not seen either of them.

An ailment would explain Meg's distress also. She must be concerned about Helena's health.

Lucien burst into Helena's bedchamber. Silence.

"Helena?" he asked. "Helena?"

He searched but did not find her. Lucien's breath hitched. She did not seem to be anywhere—but she must be. Maybe she had taken a ride—

His gaze swept over her writing desk and to the letter that bore his name. Simply *Lucien*. A strange stillness overcame him. When he walked to the desk, it was as if he were a man caught in some witch's spell. With scarcely a conscious thought, he reached for the letter and opened it.

Lucien read the words, and his heart dropped like a stone. She had gone. Helena had left, and she had taken Edmund with her. The woman—his wife—believed herself to be the architect of his ruin. Lucien closed his eyes and inhaled deeply, his senses consumed by the scent of her. The familiar lavender and rose oil still mingled in the air, and, if he had not held in his hand the evidence of her departure, he might have believed that she would return at any moment.

His chest ached, imagining Helena entering behind him and laughing, chastising him for being so worried over nothing at all.

When he opened his eyes, Lucien was still alone. He folded the letter again, caressing the paper as if, by treating it gently, he might manage to keep a part of her with him.

Meg must have known all day, and she had said nothing. Lucien tucked the letter reverently into his jacket pocket and stormed downstairs. It did not take long to find her, for she had just returned from the village. He recalled a vague conversation about Meg going to make some purchases on behalf of the estate, and he dared hope that this had all been a clever ruse. Perhaps Helena had not truly fled but merely gone to the village.

"Meg!" he snapped.

She paused at the doorway, her coat dangling from one arm. "Your Grace," she greeted, curtseying.

"Where is she?" Lucien demanded. "Where is my wife?"

"I do not know, Your Grace."

"When did she leave?" he asked. "How long has she been gone?"

How much time have I lost already?

Meg hesitated. "She must have gone sometime during the night."

"You knew," Lucien said.

"Of course I did."

"You knew, and you said nothing!" Lucien snapped, his face warming. "You knew that she was gone, and you might have said something! I could have gone after her!"

Meg defiantly tipped up her chin. "Yes, I might have, but Helena asked me not to tell you that she had gone. She wanted you to realise it yourself."

All the air left his lungs. Meg could not have wounded him more if she had caught him unaware and struck him in the stomach.

"If you had told me, I might have followed her! I might have—"

"Helena did not wish for you to follow her," Meg interrupted. "If she had wanted that, she would not have bid me keep my silence."

"But why did you?" Lucien asked. "Do you have any idea how treacherous the road will be for a lone woman and a child?"

"Of course I know!" Meg snapped. "I care for Helena, too! It pained me to keep her secret, but I owe her my loyalty!"

Lucien curled his hands into fists, his breath coming quickly. As much as he wanted to be angry with Meg, regret slowly and steadily overcame his fury.

"I apologise, Your Grace," Meg said haltingly. "I did not mean to speak so discourteously to you."

"So candidly," he said, absent-mindedly. "No—I cannot blame you for being loyal to Helena."

After Sir Bertram, there was only one person to blame, and that was himself. He should have been kinder and more patient. He should have acted more strongly—struck decisively rather than merely reacting to Sir Bertram.

"I will find her," he said, "and bring her home."

"She has many hours ahead of you, Your Grace," Meg said, her brow furrowed.

If Helena had not borrowed a horse, he should overtake her easily on horseback. But what if some misfortune had befallen her already? Lucien swallowed hard. Ravensgrave was remote, and the roads were usually safe; yet what if highwaymen happened to be passing through? What if Helena had fallen on a patch of ice and were lying wounded somewhere? What if the cold were too great?

"I do not care," he said. "I must find her. Tell Lady Honora that I will return by dinnertime."

Lucien nearly ran to the stables and rocked back on his heels, impatiently waiting as one of the stableboys deftly saddled Apollo, the fastest horse Lucien owned. Upon arriving, he had tried to saddle the horse himself, but he found that his hands shook too badly. He fumbled with the straps until giving up with a frustrated curse.

"He is ready, Your Grace," the stableboy said.

"Thank you."

He coaxed the horse into a trot. Then, a canter. Lucien decided to search the village first. If Helena had been earnest in her desire to leave, it made sense that she would go there first. If he did not find her there, he would try the trails they had ridden together. Then, the nearby forests.

He would turn the entire dukedom upside down if it might mean finding her.

***

"I have not seen Her Grace in weeks."

"Nor have I."

"Should we have seen the duchess, Your Grace? Is there something amiss?"

The villagers' replies were all different, but they came together in a cacophony that betrayed the devastating truth: no one had seen Helena. Lucien turned the horse about and continued in the opposite direction, up the road that wove through the hills and forests surrounding Ravensgrave.

If she had gone that way, there was no village for several leagues, and he imagined that he would cross her on the road. He urged Apollo into a canter, moving as quickly as he dared without overly tiring the animal. Still, there was no sign of Helena.

Nor was she in any of her familiar haunts. It was as if she had simply vanished into thin air, another ghost lost to Ravensgrave. At nightfall, he was forced to return to the estate. He dragged himself wearily to the entrance.

"Nephew." His head snapped up and found Aunt Honora standing at the top of the stairs, as regal and unruffled as ever.

"Someday, you must teach me the secret to your famous poise," he said.

Her lips curled into a dry smile. "I assume you did not find her."

"No," Lucien said. "I assume she did not return home."

"No."

The silence between them stretched, and Lucien sighed. "This is my fault," he muttered.

"It is," Aunt Honora said. "You never should have married her. I told you that it was a terrible idea."

Lucien shook his head. "Marrying Helena was not the mistake. Failing to protect her from Sir Bertram was where I erred, but I shall do something now."

Aunt Honora narrowed her eyes. "You need to think rationally about this matter. Helena is gone. You could easily request an annulment, and—"

"Never," Lucien said, stepping to the banister.

His aunt gazed coldly at him. "Do not be overly sentimental. It will be to your detriment."

"It is not sentiment. Helena deserves to be protected, and I will protect her. I have allies. Even if I do not know who they all are, I will write to them, and I will bury Sir Bertram if it takes every shred of influence I have left."

She inhaled sharply. "You just cannot leave the matter be, can you?"

"No, I cannot. I will find Helena, and I will restore her reputation. Sir Bertram cannot do this to her—especially,

especially because he has used her to hurt me. There is nothing more cowardly than using a man's wife to ruin him."

Aunt Honora sighed, looking suddenly weary beyond measure. "I know it is pointless to try and dissuade you."

"Good. Have dinner sent to me."

Lucien went to his study, pulling the door closed behind him. His eyes swept, unthinkingly, to the copy of Marcus Aurelius's writings, where Helena had scrawled her ivy in the margins. Rather than taking the volume in hand, as he might have in the past, he went to his desk and gathered several sheets of paper.

And then he wrote—letter after letter—to every potential ally. By the start of the Season, everyone in the *ton* was going to be worshipping his wife. He would make that happen, or die trying.

Chapter Twenty-Six

"This way, Mrs. Hargrove."

Helena obediently followed the matron of the boarding house up the narrow set of stairs, which creaked with every step. Edmund came last, moving with a youthful, loud energy that seemed somehow ill-suited to the place.

"You are fortunate," the matron said. "We only have one room left."

"Fortunate, indeed," Helena murmured, absent-mindedly.

She spoke of the room, but privately she let the relief of remaining unrecognised sweep over her. While Helena had hoped that the people in town would not realise that she was the Duchess of Ravensgrave, the risk had still seemed great. Thus far, she had drawn no attention, however.

She had enough money to spend a fortnight at the boarding house. Then Helena would have to decide what to do next. "Have you been in Yorkshire for long?" the matron asked.

"Not very long."

The matron opened a door to a plain, simple room. A single bed shared space with a small writing desk and a ragged chest of drawers. By the cracked window, there sat a pitcher and basin for washing. The porcelain was chipped.

"This part of the country is usually quiet," the matron continued. "Of late, the entire town is awash with rumours, though. The Duchess of Ravensgrave has seemingly had an affair with another gentleman."

Edmund inhaled sharply, and the matron cast him a concerned look. "Are you well?"

"Yes!" he exclaimed.

"I am certain that my brother is only tired," Helena said. "It has been a long journey for the both of us."

East Falls was a market town two days east of Ravensgrave. While it was nothing near London, Helena had thought that it might be a pleasant enough place to hide if one wished. She could not quite decide if she was hiding. It was more that she did not wish to be found quite yet, although she knew that Lucien must be searching for her.

Helena searched the matron's face, concerned that Edmund's reaction might have aroused suspicion, but the woman only nodded, her face soft with sympathy.

"I shall leave you both to settle in."

"Thank you," Helena said.

Once the matron closed the door behind her, Helena sagged in relief against the wood. Edmund bounded onto the bed, which creaked alarmingly beneath his slight weight. A cool wind stirred lightly within the room, bringing a great cloud of damp with it. Edmund said nothing.

Helena sighed deeply. "There are worse places that we could stay."

She thought of the dilapidated nursery that Edmund had first stayed in at Ravensgrave. At least this room had not borne the brunt of fire damage. It was clean and neat, if a little sparse. The draught was undesirable, but at least they had shelter. That was more than many could say.

"We shall make the best of it," Helena added, trying to sound optimistic.

She wanted to say that she had already considered all other options and that this was the best one, that she had a plan for what to do next, but both of those statements would be lies. Leaving had been a choice, one that she had thought about for a long time. It would be best for Lucien.

But maybe not for her. Maybe not for Edmund.

"We always do," Edmund said softly.

He seemed to hold a hesitation so deeply that Helena's heart ached for him. Edmund gazed at her as if one wrong word might cause her to break into pieces.

"Yes," Helena said, sighing.

Would it have been better for her to have left Edmund at Ravensgrave with Meg? Her brother's only misfortune was in being her sibling, but his name had not yet appeared in the pamphlets or scandal sheets. She was certain that Lucien would have taken good care of him if he had stayed.

Perhaps, even better care than she could. Helena forced down the lump that rose in her throat.

"I need to visit the printer's shop that we passed on the way here," Helena said. "The matron mentioned gossip about me, and I would like to know what is being said in town."

She hoped dearly that the gossip had ceased, but she doubted that it had. If anything, Helena imagined that it had become even more insidious, as different writers took what they read and added to it. With every telling, the rumours would become more lurid, and as long as the scandal sheets made a profit, the stories would only grow.

"Should... should I come with you?"

Helena smiled gently. "No," she said. "I think I should do this on my own. Rest. It has been a trying few months for you."

"For you, too."

"Yes, but I am…" She trailed off. "I am older, so I have more responsibilities than you do."

Edmund slowly nodded and spread across the bed, which groaned with every movement. Helena stifled a sigh, her eyes drifting over the threadbare bed linens and the scratched, dented bedframe.

"I will return soon," she said. "I promise."

"I know."

Helena fidgeted with her cloak. She felt as if she ought to say something more to her brother, but she could not find the words for all the emotions whirling about like a tempest inside her. What would her parents have done in this situation? Would they have stayed at Ravensgrave and borne the scandal?

Her chest ached. Lucien would certainly have discovered her absence already. Would he be upset or relieved? Would he try to seek her out? Helena suspected that he would, but she found herself unable to decide if his pursuit would be out of love or duty.

She gave Edmund a small, parting smile. "It will be fine," Helena said.

As she bounded down the creaking stairs, she could not decide if she was trying to reassure her brother or herself. She hurried from the boarding house, her heart beating quite quickly as she wove through the streets to the printer's shop. It was, fortunately, not far away.

Her breath caught in her throat as she surveyed the pamphlets and scandal sheets proudly displayed through the printer's glass storefront. *Scandal in Ravensgrave* declared one pamphlet. Helena curled her hands into fists, her mind awhirl. Even though she had anticipated the printer's having some of the familiar scandal sheets, seeing them with her own eyes was another matter entirely.

Helena exhaled raggedly, her blood roaring in her ears. Her own name was printed in stark black ink. *The Duchess of Ravensgrave, Helena Ashmore...*

She could only read the first page of the scandal sheet, but the story was sufficiently lurid from the first paragraph. This author had speculated that her marriage to Lucien was a thinly veiled attempt to make Sir Bertram jealous, hoping that he would desire her long after his own passion had faded into nothingness.

"Absurd!" she whispered.

But would it be absurd to the *ton*? She thought of Lady Alwood, who had warned her about Sir Bertram's plans. That lady would not readily believe such lies, would she? Even if some of the *ton* believed the gossip, there must be some who would not, who would realise that Lucien had been the unfortunate victim of some petty man's slander.

But will that be enough?

The door to the printer's shop swung open, and a young man peered from within. "Did you need something, Miss?"

"No," she replied, smiling tightly. "I apologise. I did not mean to linger. It was only that I observed the rather sensational headline, and..."

Helena hoped that he would assume she was only a curious passer-by, and he seemed to, for he nodded with a look of wry understanding. "Her Grace has certainly made the town lively," he said. "But the Ashmores have long been a source of interest for the town."

"Oh?"

"Yes, the family seems cursed. At least, that is what my mother says. They say that the late duke drank himself to death and, in a drunken fit, set the estate ablaze," the man said. "And before that, there was the—the elder son, who died in a duel."

She had not known those things. Lucien had never told her. Why not? Had he not trusted her? Helena furrowed her brow. A longing for Lucien swept over her, so fierce and sudden that her knees were weak.

"Unfortunate, indeed," Helena murmured. "But I suspect the duchess was cursed long before she married Lu—the duke."

"Seemingly so," the young man said, shaking his head ruefully. "If you want to buy one of the pamphlets, you can read all about it. She's supposedly a murderess."

"Perhaps next time," Helena said. "Thank you, though."

Without awaiting his reply, she hurried away, trudging through the muddied street. There were so many pamphlets and scandal sheets in the window! It seemed inconceivable that they would all be purchased. There must be more important things happening in the world than her scandals, but it seemed as though the people of East Falls did not think so.

She entered the boarding house with a huff, giving a quick and forced smile to the matron, who glanced up from the book she was reading. What would Helena do once the fortnight had passed? She dared to imagine what it would be like to flee to some far-flung place, like Scotland or Ireland, where no one knew her face or name. It would be just a simple matter of taking Edmund with her and heading northward. They could start anew. It would be difficult without even references, but it would be possible.

They had managed everything else.

She climbed the stairs, her mind in some perilous place between defeat and defiance. If she fled to Scotland or Ireland, she and Edmund would survive, but she could not say that it would be a happy existence. And Lucien...

Her chest ached. If she did not act, Lucien would have to fight this fire on his own.

She pulled open the door to the room. Edmund rolled onto his side and stared at her, his face pale in the gathering gloom of twilight. "Did you find what you wanted?" he asked.

"I found what I expected." She tried to sound flippant and unaffected, as though her scandals were not growing like mistletoe and threatening to choke her beneath their weight. "It is nothing to worry about."

"Good," Edmund said.

Helena could not decide if her brother sounded disbelieving or if she had only imagined the tremor in his voice.

"Try not to let all of this distress you," Helena said softly. "We have endured more than our share of misfortune, but this shall pass, too."

"I know."

The silence between them grew. Helena walked to the writing desk and lowered herself into the chair. The sight of her name in that stark, black print still lingered at the forefront of her mind, like an omen of ill will.

She needed to stop the flood of pamphlets before she drowned beneath them. Helena sighed deeply and ran her hand through her hair, fingers snagging on pins. What could she do? She supposed that she might have some legal recourse, but she did not quite know what form that might take. She thought of Mr Hart and his nervous manner. Could she trust such a man to understand her plight?

Worse, could she trust him not to judge her? Helena could not bear having a man look at her, judge her, and decide her guilt all in a glance. Besides, what if he made a mess of things?

No—

She must do something to settle this matter herself. Helena eyed the blank pieces of paper, stacked neatly on the desk. A pen and ink waited beside them; the items looked as though they had never been touched. She bit her lip.

Perhaps part of the problem was that Sir Bertram's words were the only account of events in circulation. Once, she had been a writer—not the best, but adequate. Maybe it was time for her to seize the narrative and take control.

Helena dipped the pen in ink and pressed it against the page. *The Anatomy of a Scandal,* she wrote.

If Sir Bertram wished to fight this war with words, it was long past time that he had a proper opponent.

Chapter Twenty-Seven

Lucien was a careful man, but this situation required some boldness. The Mayleigh Assembly always met at the Hawthorne Estate, historically owned by the Viscount of Berkley. In recent years, it had fallen into the hands of the notorious gossip Mrs Eleanor Langley. She was a widow, dripping with more wealth than most of the *ton* and twice as much influence. Mrs Langley was the only woman ever to be asked to host such an assembly, and it was she who had received Lucien's first letter.

He had planned to arrive with the truth. By happenstance, Meg had given him another pamphlet, *The Anatomy of a Scandal*, that morning. He had read it, nearly breathless. When he reached the end and found that the piece was signed by Helena Ashmore, Duchess of Ravensgrave, all air left his lungs. His brazen wife had published a rebuttal. He supposed that he ought to have expected that.

As he entered the ballroom, Mrs Langley cast him a sly glance. She was an older woman, in her late fifties or early sixties, but she carried her age well. The woman snapped a fan and smiled, her brown eyes bright with delight in anticipation of the scene soon to unfold. "Your Grace," she said. "You have arrived late."

"Indeed, I have."

"I do so love a dramatic entrance," she said. "You have promised me theatre tonight. I hope you do not disappoint."

"I shall not."

His eyes swept over the ballroom, quickly finding Sir Bertram amongst the crowd. The man stood surrounded by gentlemen. Some were former allies. Lucien clenched his jaw. So much for loyalty.

Peter Langford stood across the ballroom. Their eyes met, and Lucien strode to him. He feigned as though their interaction were merely casual, just a small exchange of smiles. Then he withdrew a bundle from his jacket.

"This is most unusual, Your Grace," Langford said.

"I know."

Langford took the bundle without another word and tucked it into his own jacket, waiting for the best moment to reveal its contents to the *ton.*

He continued his circuit around the ballroom until he reached Beatrice. His cousin smiled at him, waving her fan in a slow, mischievous manner. When she snapped it shut, Lucien spied the familiar folded pamphlet held in place by the sticks. It was Helena's work, *The Anatomy of a Scandal.*

"For you," Beatrice said, grinning.

He plucked the pamphlet from her fan. "Soon, the show will begin," he said.

"Aunt Honora will be displeased that you have chosen to resolve the scandal in this manner."

"Undoubtedly," Lucien agreed. "But it matters not. I have decided upon this course of action, and I will not abandon it now."

"The waltz will end soon," Beatrice said.

He nodded. Lucien clasped his hands behind his back, the pamphlet held tightly between his fingers. The dancers twirled in time with the lively music. With each note, anticipation coiled more tightly inside him.

Lucien was all too aware of how badly this plan might go, but he also knew that, if he succeeded, Mrs Langley would ensure that all Britain knew the truth before sunrise.

The song ended, and Mrs Langley stepped forward, applauding. "A fine dance!" she declared.

Heads turned towards her, the room suddenly absorbed in the hostess's words. Lucien straightened his spine, knowing that the woman's verdict was soon to come.

"I believe that we are all owed an explanation," Mrs Langley said, "and perhaps an apology."

"Best of luck," Beatrice murmured.

"Luck? I have no need for that. I have Helena's words, after all."

Lucien stepped away from Beatrice and held the pamphlet aloft for all to see. Heads turned towards him, eyes snapping to his face as he approached the centre of the ballroom. "You are correct, Mrs Langley. I believe that an apology is owed to my wife and me."

Sir Bertram, still standing among his allies, raised an eyebrow. The man's face was insufferably smug, as if daring Lucien to continue. He hardly needed a man to tempt his words, for indignation burned inside him. Sir Bertram had sought to ruin Helena time and time again for his own selfish gain, and Lucien would ensure that such schemes ended at once.

"Some of you are aware of the cruel pamphlets which have been circulating about my wife Helena. You have read the scandal sheets, too. Tonight, I intend to reveal the truth of everything that has happened," Lucien said. "If you have read *The Anatomy of a Scandal*, you already know that the true villain is not my wife. Instead, it is a vile and selfish man, who stands among you now—Sir Bertram."

Sir Bertram laughed, the sound echoing in the otherwise silent room. "Your Grace, I understand that you are upset about this scandal, but—"

"I am upset only because you have besmirched my good wife," Lucien cut in. "This pamphlet details everything. You wished to marry Helena, but she had no interest in wedding you. When she denied you and rebuffed your advances, you sought to be the architect of her ruin."

Sir Bertram shook his head in what Lucien perceived to be feigned dismay. "I am certain that is what she told you, but I fear that you have been misled, Your Grace. Your wife also misled me when she offered me reconciliation with you. I do not know how she has tried to explain herself, but she lies, as distasteful as that may be to believe of one's wife. I notice that the lady is not here to speak for herself. Perhaps she realised the futility of such a task."

Lucien clenched his jaw, but then he remembered the importance of the moment and forced himself to relax. "Helena has nothing to hide," he said smoothly. "But you have much to conceal. When you perceived me as a threat to your power, you sought to ruin me. The *ton* whispered that I did not have a wife, and once I found one, you were displeased with my choice. You knew you must devise some other means to ruin me, so you decided to use Helena against me. You orchestrated her ruin in an attempt to ruin my own reputation!"

"Absurd," Sir Bertram said.

"Perhaps," Lady Alwood said. "What proof do you have, Your Grace?"

Lucien sensed that she did not entirely believe Sir Bertram, and he seized upon the opportunity the lady presented. "Sir

Bertram wrote the pamphlet about Helena, lying about her past. He also created the recent scandal sheet, which alleges that Helena lured him to a small village near Ravensgrave with the intention of seducing him. Helena has written about all of this in her own pamphlet, which has been verified by others."

"I do not see how that can be," Sir Bertram said, "since Her Grace lies."

"She does not," Lucien insisted. "But I thought you might wish to contest my claims, so I ensured that I had proof of them for tonight."

Langford cleared his throat. "I have a signed confession from one of the men who testified to seeing Her Grace speaking with you, Sir Bertram, in the village."

Sir Bertram's easy smile faltered just a little. "We already know what the witnesses said. Their statements were published in the scandal sheets."

"Were they?" Langford asked. "That is very interesting, because this one says—and I quote—*I admit to speaking to a gentleman and admitting that I had seen Her Grace speaking to Sir Bertram in an intimate manner. However, this confession was not made of my own volition. Although I did see Her Grace's encounter with Sir Bertram, I would describe the meeting as cold and combative. It was apparent to me that the duchess was startled by his arrival, and I do not believe that the meeting was arranged.*"

"One man's account," Sir Bertram said.

"The account continues," Langford said. "This man alleges being threatened by your valet, hence why he slandered the Duchess of Ravensgrave. He feared for his safety and had no other recourse. When I tried to verify his account, he admitted this all quite readily to me."

233

Sir Bertram shook his head. "No," he said. "No, this is some trap of yours. It is quite apparent that you hope to discredit me, so you have concocted this entire story to convince the *ton* that I am the deceitful one!"

"But there is more," Beatrice said. "We also have obtained a statement from the printer, Mr Finch, who alleges that you persuaded him to defame the duchess. You threatened him with financial ruin if he would not do as you wished."

Sir Bertram's nostrils flared. His face twitched, as though he found it difficult to maintain his easy façade. Lucien smiled grimly. It seemed as though the plan was working. Sir Bertram was unravelling before their very eyes, and if Lucien just pushed a little more, the whole *ton* would witness it. He could restore Helena's reputation!

"Desperate lies!" exclaimed Sir Bertram, glancing about him in what seemed to be a desperate search for supporters. "I would never do something so heinous!"

"But you would," Lucien said, withdrawing a paper from his jacket. "I have an invoice from Mr Finch, bearing your name, and the date matches the exact date that Helena met with you. Admit it! You orchestrated that meeting and smeared her reputation with it! I have it here for anyone who wishes to inspect it."

The *ton* whispered excitedly amongst themselves. Mrs Langley approached and extended her hand, as imperious as any queen. Lucien tilted the paper into her waiting palm.

"What do you think? I believe that paper supports my claims well enough! This man conspired against my wife, spread dreadful rumours to ruin her reputation, and all for his own selfish gain! He wrote lies and buried the truth for votes!"

Mrs Langley hummed, her lips pursed into a thin line. Lucien could sense her intentions. She enjoyed having everyone watching her, waiting with bated breath to see if he could truly deliver all that he had said.

"Well," Mrs Langley said at last. "The matter is quite clear to me. Sir Bertram, I imagine you will be leaving now."

The room seemed to collectively inhale. Sir Bertram only smiled. "This is nothing," he said, "but a baseless political ambush. A theatrical production."

Lucien arched an eyebrow, noting that the gentlemen who had previously stood close to Sir Bertram had shifted further away. The *ton*'s whispers grew, and they were unkind. With a mocking bow to Mrs Langley, Sir Bertram stormed from the ballroom.

"I doubt that you have seen the last of him," Mrs Langley warned, returning the invoice to Lucien. "Do be careful, Your Grace."

"Indeed, I shall be. Thank you for all your assistance regarding this matter."

He did not stay to celebrate his victory, for he had more important tasks at hand. Lucien had only been apart from Helena for a handful of days, but even that small time apart felt as though it were an eternity. He needed to find her. Fortunately, he had a good idea where she must have gone. Her pamphlet had reached Ravensgrave with such remarkable speed that she must be dwelling near a printer's shop and within a short distance of Ravensgrave, and the only printer's shop nearby was in East Falls, only two days away.

Chapter Twenty-Eight

Rain fell in sharp, merciless droplets, and Helena, who had spent the better part of the morning trying to keep herself from becoming too wet in the insistent downpour, finally accepted defeat. She ducked beneath a tree and made no further efforts to protect herself from the onslaught of rain. Helena shivered through her cloak and gown. A small part of her ached for the warmth of Ravensgrave and for Lucien's affection.

The rain was so fierce that it had soaked through her boots and her stockings, reminding her acutely of that first day when she had met Lucien. She closed her eyes and breathed, inhaling the sharpness of tree bark and the freshness of rain. Now, Lucien was gone.

"Helena!"

She almost cried in despair, for she swore that she heard his voice carried on the wind. Helena blinked back rainwater and slowly sank to the ground, the wet seeping through the fabric of her skirts. She pulled her knees up and let her forehead rest atop them. Her eyes burned with tears, and she made no effort to stop them. Helena shivered and shuddered, her breath coming in hot and uncomfortable gasps for air.

She should never have married Lucien. Helena had only brought him ruin, and she had selfishly remained for far longer than she should have. If she had never wed him, he would have eventually found another bride, one who was more suitable than she!

"Helena!"

"Again?" she exclaimed, despair sweeping through her.

The man haunted her even two days away from Ravensgrave! She swore that she heard his voice carried upon the wind.

"Helena!" A gasp followed. "God, Helena!"

Her head snapped up, and her breath caught in her throat. All Helena's thoughts came to a sudden halt. Lucien stood before her, his hair darkened with rainwater. His face was flushed, his lips slightly parted, and every breath he drew seemed to send a shudder through his entire body. He took a tentative step forward, wet fabric clinging to him. Lucien extended a hand to her, as though he thought she might be some illusion, and feared that she might vanish if he approached her too suddenly.

He must be a dream—or, failing that, a vision conjured by the recent taxing experiences on her nerves. Helena opened her mouth to speak, for even a vision of Lucien was preferable to not having him at all, but no words emerged.

His breath cut through the air in a loud whoosh, and he dropped to the ground before her. Lucien's arms wrapped around her, holding her tight. "I have you, my dearest."

He was wet and cold, as was Helena, but still she drew warmth from his strength. Lucien was there. He was real.

"You found me," she whispered, her throat raw.

"Of course I did."

She allowed herself one heartbeat longer in his embrace. Then she pushed him away. Lucien faltered a little, nearly losing his balance. He caught himself on his hands and stared at her as if she had taken leave of her senses.

"Go," Helena said. "You should not be here. You should not have come after me. I made my choice, and I wanted to leave."

Lucien furrowed his brow. "Did you?"

"Yes. I do not wish to be your burden," Helena said. "Don't you see? If you had not come after me, you could have claimed that I abandoned you. You could have annulled the marriage."

Lucien leaned forward and pressed his lips against hers. It was a light and gentle kiss, barely there, but it still left Helena breathless.

"Why would I want to do either of those things?" he asked, pressing his forehead against her own. "You are my wife, and I love you. I have taken great efforts to restore your reputation. Why would I do all of that if I did not wish to keep you as my duchess and my wife?"

"What are you talking about?"

"I received your pamphlet and read it at Mrs Langley's ball. You would not know her, but she is a notorious gossip. We arranged a... theatrical production, so to speak. I sent Langford to find the source of the pamphlets, and he received an invoice from Mr Finch. Beatrice went to the village and asked around until she found the men who said they saw your meeting with Sir Bertram, and she and Langford persuaded them both to admit that they had lied. We revealed all of it. We buried Sir Bertram, and you won, Helena. Everyone knows that he sought to ruin you for his own selfish gain."

It all sounded too good to be true. Helena roughly rubbed her hands against her eyes. "You really did that? But you could have been rid of me."

"Of course I did. I love you, Helena."

She slumped against him, burying her face in the crook of his neck. Lucien held her tightly and held her for a long time. After her tears ceased, he squeezed her hand. "Shall I make you feel better?" he asked.

It was an echo of the last time they had made love, when she had gratefully lost herself in his touch. He guided Helena to her feet. Rain dripped down the sides of her face, and she pressed herself close to Lucien. A few paces from the road, just at the forest's edge, was a house nearly consumed by ivy. He stepped inside, taking her with him. The roof was entirely gone, weathered away long ago by the elements. Above them, grey clouds rolled.

Helena stepped gingerly over the broken stone floor. Lucien lowered his head and kissed the side of her neck, and Helena's breath hitched. She pressed her thighs together in anticipation of the pleasure soon to come. He pressed her against the wall and bent his knees slightly. Lucien hitched her skirts up, his movements slow and careful. She almost laughed at the absurdity of his care, for her skirts were sodden and beyond saving, the dark blue dye bleeding onto the ground and gathering in little puddles.

At last, his hands cupped her thighs. "Up," he whispered against her throat.

With a grunt, he hefted her upwards. Helena gasped and wrapped her legs around his waist. She put her hands on his shoulders, keeping herself steady. Her back pressed against the wall. "Like this?" she gasped.

A low laugh rumbled in his chest. "Yes. Just like this, Helena."

He squeezed her thighs, his thumbs rubbing circles along her bare skin. Above them, thunder roared. Lucien leaned his body against hers, so there was no space between them. Already, his manhood stirred with interest; Helena felt it hard against her stomach.

Her toes curled in her boots, all thoughts of discomfort gone in the warmth of Lucien's breath against her throat, the softness of his hands on her thighs, and the joy blooming in her chest at her husband having found her at last. And he loved her. He had restored her reputation for her. For them.

"I love you," she murmured, kissing his cheek. "I love you so much."

"I do not deserve you."

He trailed kisses along her jaw and down to her throat; every press of his lips against her skin was like coming home after a long journey. Helena groaned and dug her fingers into his damp hair. Her hips jolted against Lucien, drawing a ragged cry from him.

"You feel so good against me," Lucien said. "I have missed everything about you—your brilliance, your wit, your touch—and I hope and pray that you will return to Ravensgrave with me."

"Yes!"

Heat pulsed in her core, and her thighs trembled. She lowered one hand to his trousers, frantically unfastening them. Her fingers brushed against his manhood, and her breath caught in her chest. Helena experimentally took hold of him, wrapping her hand around his cockstand.

"Ooh, Helena," he murmured, his voice raw. "Take care, or I will spend before I even enter you."

She did not want that, for Helena desired pleasure of her own, but the thought of seeing her husband come undone because of her touch awakened a heat that she had never felt before. Helena carefully adjusted herself, so his manhood found her entrance.

"Are you ready?" he asked, brushing his nose over the curve of her breasts.

"Yes," she breathed.

With one jolt of his hips, he was inside her. Helena tossed her head back and gasped. He entered steadily, inch by inch. Her muscles all drew tight, and her body reflexively moved to meet his. She recognised his rhythm and worked to keep pace with him. Helena's hips bucked to meet his every thrust. They moved in unison, their bodies moving together as if they were one. Her breath quickened, her panting breaths mingling with the low rumble of the thunder and the persistent beat of rain.

As her release built between her legs, Helena felt as though she was the centre of the universe, as though she and the elements had become one. Lucien groaned. His muscles drew taut, and his thighs quivered. Lucien grasped her legs so firmly that Helena gasped, startled. A flood of warmth jolted in her thighs, and Helena screamed in pleasure. Her own release swept over her in a rush of white light. In the aftermath, she clung to Lucien and pressed her forehead into his shoulder.

The beating rain was no longer unpleasant. Instead, it helped soothe the feverish warmth of her skin. "Thank you," Helena said. "Thank you for this. Thank you for coming after me."

Lucien drew his right hand down her thigh, slowly helping her to her feet. Helena's knees shook. Her core pulsed in satisfaction. If he had been willing and able, she would have happily taken him again. Instead, he drew her into his arms, folding her against him.

"Of course I did. I would have torn Britain apart until I found you."

She laughed. "I would never ask that of you."

"I would never make you ask."

He kissed her again, low and lingering. Helena smiled at him, watching the raindrops fall down the sides of his face. "We are both so wet," she said.

He chuckled and cast his eyes upwards to the grey clouds. "So we are. Do you want to return to your lodgings?"

"Not yet."

Lucien lowered himself onto the ground and extended a hand to Helena. "You are ridiculous," she said.

"You are the one who did not wish to return yet."

He stretched out over the broken floor and grinned mischievously. With a sly smile, Helena lay beside him, pressing her cheek against his chest. Lucien wrapped his arms around her and kissed her hair. "I think it will clear soon," he murmured.

Helena looked up and observed the small slivers of light that drifted between the dark and bloated clouds. "I think you are right," she said.

"It will certainly be gone by the time we return to Ravensgrave."

Helena inhaled softly. "Yes."

"I have missed you."

"And I have missed you."

"Will you promise never to leave me again?" Lucien asked. "No matter what may come?"

"Yes," she said. "I promise."

And she meant it. Despite all the distressing events that had unfolded over the past several weeks, she was safe in Lucien's arms. He was her home, as much as Ravensgrave was, and Helena never wanted to leave him again. For the first time since her father's death, Helena was at peace.

Chapter Twenty-Nine

Six Weeks Later

Laughter and music threaded lightly through the grand ballroom of Ravensgrave, which until recently had not seen usage in many years. Helena, who had planned the event with considerable aid from Beatrice and Meg, took a small sip from her glass of champagne. She glanced at Lucien. He stood beside her, steady and calm. "Are you ready?" he asked.

Helena gathered her courage and nodded. "Yes."

Lucien inclined his head to her, his face softening. It was strange to remember that she had once found him imposing, that she had considered him someone who might be frightening.

The music ended, and the dancing couples bowed and curtsied to one another. Helena took a deep breath and stepped into the centre of the ballroom, raising her glass. She waited as the laughter and conversations slowly died around her. Soon, all eyes were on her.

Helena's heartbeat quickened. She found the familiar faces in the crowd. Lucien, first. But there was Beatrice standing near Mr Langford. Edmund lingered at the edge of the ballroom; he had not wished to attend, but he had wanted to hear her speech. Meg lingered behind him. As the new stewardess of Ravensgrave, she had overseen most of the day with admirable efficiency. There were other welcome faces, like Lady Alwood, who had flashed her an approving smile upon her arrival.

And one face—Lady Honora—was entirely absent. After Helena's return to Ravensgrave, the woman had quietly packed her possessions and left. She had been unwilling to live with such a scandalous woman any longer, and it seemed that Lucien's working to restore Helena's reputation had—somehow, paradoxically—left Lady Honora feeling as though the present situation was intolerable. Helena could not help but feel a little relieved when she came down for breakfast each morning and found the woman absent. She had not realised just how difficult it was to breathe with Lady Honora about until she was gone. Still, there was another part of Helena that regretted she had never been able to win the affections of Lucien's aunt. Lady Honora was a strong and wilful woman, and in other circumstances, she and Helena might have been friends.

Helena raised her glass, smiling. "Friends and acquaintances," she said. "Thank you so much for joining us on this joyous night. I am told that this is the first ball to be held at Ravensgrave for many years."

She knew that it was. There had been no balls since Lucien's brother Henry died, something which he had finally spoken to her about in the weeks following her return to Ravensgrave.

"I would like to claim credit for this beautiful ballroom and how splendidly the occasion is, but I cannot in good conscience do so, for I did very little. Much of the credit for this beautiful night belongs to my cousin Lady Beatrice and my efficient stewardess, Meg. And of course, to my indulgent husband."

The comment received a small titter of laughs. Lady Alwood whispered something to Lord Alwood, a sly smirk stretched across her face. The infamous Mrs Langley raised her fan and cast Helena a mischievous glance above it.

"Tonight, I want to speak of the importance of resilience. The world can be a cold and careless place, especially for ladies. So much depends upon our reputations, but our value may be ruined by something as small as one disgruntled suitor."

245

Helena paused, waiting to see how the words were received. Seeing several respectful nods, especially from the ladies, gave her the courage to continue. "I want to dedicate this night in celebration of all those ladies and gentlemen who have been unjustly besmirched, especially while in the pursuit of doing good."

Lady Alwood applauded, a gesture which was soon taken up by the rest of the guests. Helena waited for the applause to cease. Her eyes darted to Lucien, who stood at the edge of the ballroom. Helena's husband was half cast in shadow, but the flickering flame-light was enough to see his gentle smile.

"I hope that tonight will usher in a new era for Ravensgrave," Helena continued. "Let our estate and our lives be a testament to the possibility of change, of the old being made new. And for those of you who might not have already read my pamphlet *The Anatomy of a Scandal*, I have it here tonight. My reason for sharing this pamphlet is not a spiteful one. I have no desire to humiliate Sir Bertram for slandering my reputation; such a base cause as revenge would be inappropriate. I wish only for the truth to be known and for others to take appropriate caution in their dealings with Sir Bertram."

Edmund took a silver platter, laden with pamphlets, from Meg's waiting hands. Together, the two of them spread throughout the ballroom. Helena's heart fluttered with satisfaction. It had been an arduous journey to reveal the truth to everyone, but at last, she had. Everyone knew that Sir Bertram was a villain, and she need not be plagued by him any longer.

She raised her champagne flute once more, toasting her guests, and took a long drink. Then she stepped lightly from the centre of the room. The orchestra, recognising their cue, began to play once more. Helena walked to Lucien, who bowed. He took her hand and kissed her knuckles, sending her heart racing.

"I would ask if I did well," Helena said, "but I already know that I did."

Lucien chuckled. "I am glad," he said. "Your event has gone rather nicely, and I could not be more pleased for you. My sweet Helena, marrying you was by far the best decision that I ever made."

"Even though you were forced to endure so much for my sake?" she asked.

"Yes," he said. "Everything that I endure was worth it if it means that I have the privilege of waking up every morning with the knowledge that you are my wife."

Heat flooded her face, and she ducked her head. Sometimes, the warmth of his affections made her feel just a little shy. "I might say the same of you," she said.

Lucien smiled, his face softened with affection. "Shall we dance?"

"If you like."

He gallantly offered his arm, and Helena let herself be led to the dance floor. They fell seamlessly into the ring of dancers, and Helena's heart was so full of love for her husband that it seemed impossible to feel so much.

***

After the ball ended and the guests had all gone, Helena quietly slipped from the house and entered the gardens. August's wind ruffled her hair and the flowers along the path. She inhaled the sweet scent of lilacs and roses, the ravages of winter long since swept away by new growth.

New growth and a new life for her, she mused. Since Lucien had found her again in East Falls, Helena had slowly begun to think of herself more each day as the true Duchess of

Ravensgrave. No longer was she the outsider, the one who did not belong among all the lords and ladies of the *ton*. Instead, she fit in with the rest of them. She was their equal in all the ways that mattered, and Helena would have traded that feeling for nothing in the world.

A throat cleared behind her, and Helena did not need to turn to know who had followed her. "Did you enjoy the evening?" she asked.

"Immensely," Lucien said. "It was made all the better because I was celebrating your efforts."

She glanced over her shoulder at him and smiled. "It is strange that we will wake in the morning, and all our guests will be gone. We have not had a moment of quiet for weeks now."

"Yes." He paused, considering her. "However, I find that I do not think the loudness so vexing when I am with you."

She laughed. "You praise me too highly, Lucien. From how you speak, people would assume that I had put the moon in the sky."

"They would be correct," he said. "Metaphorically speaking. If you are the sun, I am content to be your moon."

Warmth slowly spread across her face. While the words were meant to be romantic, they were not quite novel, and, in truth, they did not sound much like Lucien. He might enjoy reading poetry, but crafting it with his own words was another matter entirely.

But he had tried for her, for no other reason than he thought that she might be pleased by his words.

"I do adore you, husband," she said. "You are kinder than I deserve sometimes."

"Nonsense! You have always deserved kindness. It is unfortunate that you have been so long deprived of it. I only wish that I had met you sooner, so I might have shown you what love was like earlier in your life. Perhaps I would have met you before the scandal with your father. I could have supported you through the ordeal and made it easier to bear."

"Yes," she said. "I am certain that you could have, but I do not know if I would wish the same. I love you now, and I love how our affection for one another has deepened. If I had met you earlier and not been forced to endure as I have, I am uncertain that I would have been prepared to marry you and be the wife that you deserved."

"Maybe," Lucien said.

Helena turned to face him and clasped her hands before her. Lucien smiled and stepped to her. His hands found her shoulders. He gently caressed his way down her arms. Once he reached her wrists, Lucien raised them to his lips, kissing one after the other.

"You are still as beautiful to me now as you were the day that we met."

"Thank you."

He wrapped his arms around her waist and drew her close. Lucien lowered his head and kissed her hair, giving a satisfied sigh. Helena placed a quick kiss on his jaw, just above his collar.

"Insatiable," he murmured.

"As if you are not equally so."

"I made no protestations to the contrary," he pointed out.

He tipped her chin up with a single finger and kissed her. At first, he was light and gentle—only the faintest little pressure

249

against her lips. But then he deepened the kiss. His fingers curled in her hair, and she clung to his jacket. They kissed and kissed and kissed until Helena thought that she might burst from the joy of being one with him, of being so irreversibly connected to one another.

He broke the kiss and coaxed her into retreating, so her back pressed against the stone wall behind her. She fixed him with a coy look, remembering their amorous congress in the storm in that little building just outside East Falls. Anticipation surged through her core, hot and eager. As if he knew her thoughts, Lucien heaved her skirts up. He drew his hand up her thigh, and she gasped.

Lucien grinned, his expression equal parts wicked and amused. "I believe it is time for us to go to the bedchamber, is it not?"

She had a wild thought that it might be enjoyable to engage in some manner of dalliance in the gardens, but she also knew the dangers of that. The chances that they might be caught by either Beatrice or Edmund were too great. "I think it is."

He effortlessly drew her up and into his arms, and she laughed. Helena wrapped her arms around his neck, her thumb brushing his hair. "I love you," she said.

She had said it more times than she could count, at least once a day since returning from East Falls, but somehow, all those times were never enough.

She needed to say it again and again, every day for the rest of her life.

Epilogue

One Year Later

Lucien surveyed the east wing. Once burned and uninhabitable, it had been transformed into a perfectly respectable nursery. A shelf laden with books covered one wall. Another wall proudly displayed Helena's botanical sketches, meticulously painted and labelled. Beneath the window, a chessboard—paused mid-game—sat. He and Edmund had taken to playing together almost every day. Lucien strongly suspected their games were to his detriment, for Edmund seemed to play better each time. There was little doubt that he would eventually best Lucien.

An armchair was placed in the corner, a half-finished scarf draped over the back of it. Meg had taken to reading there each night. Lucien smiled fondly.

"Mr Langford!" Beatrice's laughter drifted into the room.

Lucien smiled wryly. Although still conflicted about Aunt Honora's absence, he could not deny that Beatrice, who had insisted on remaining behind, seemed to have blossomed without their aunt always watching her. She spent long nights writing at her desk, and the stack of small, neatly written pages grew day by day. Soon, she would have her completed novel, the content of which was certain to upset Aunt Honora.

Langford's low voice rumbled, too soft for Lucien to hear the words.

"You are impossible!" Beatrice declared.

Lucien shook his head and wondered, not for the first time, if Beatrice might have some interest in Langford.

He drifted through the corridor, mostly searching for Helena. Lucien did not hurry, however, for he knew that she was somewhere in Ravensgrave. He passed the next room and slipped inside, looking towards the bed. Edmund slept peacefully, his face softened in the moonlight. A swell of affection overcame Lucien as he watched the steady rise and fall of the boy's chest. In some ways, Edmund reminded him of Henry when he was young.

"Pleasant dreams," Lucien murmured.

He continued along the corridor until he reached the stairs. Lucien descended them, accompanied by the faint sounds of Beatrice and Langford, still deep in conversation. He considered joining them but dismissed the idea just as quickly. The pair would have a chaperone, of course, but speaking together in front of a parlour maid was quite different from conversing with him, listening across the room.

He continued on, pushing open the door that opened onto the gardens. Spring had done them well. Where once there had been dead grasses and wilted blossoms, there were now bright flowers and grass that was green and lush. Helena had taken charge of revitalising them, and Lucien, who had no particular gift for coaxing plants to grow, had employed additional gardeners to aid her efforts.

Soon, everyone would appreciate Helena's gifts for tending to the plants and flowers, for she had finally thought to revisit her old manuscript. She had decided to have it published; with just a few more changes, it would be perfect. Then there would be two lady writers in the family, Beatrice and Helena.

Lucien entered the conservatory, the door repaired with new glass. Inside, the conservatory was pristine, all the plants neatly trimmed and arranged. Helena stood in the midst of it all, her feet bare.

"What are you doing?" Lucien asked.

Helena looked over her shoulder at him. She raised a hand to tuck a wayward strand of hair behind her ear. He spied ink stains on her pale hand, made more apparent in the silvery light of the moon. "I had a thought about the hedgerow."

"It is rather late to be thinking about the hedgerow. You should be resting."

His gaze drifted from her face to the swell of her stomach, which was just beginning to show through the skirts of her gown.

"You do not need to treat me like glass," she said, her hands drifting down to her stomach. "I have been resting for most of the day. It was only that I did not wish to lose the thought."

Lucien smiled. "You could have asked the gardener. I would have fetched him in the morning to come and see the hedgerow on your behalf."

"You married an independent woman," she said. "You cannot be surprised that you have what you were promised."

He wrapped his arms around Helena and kissed her, inhaling her familiar floral scent. "My dear, wonderful wife," he murmured against her mouth.

Lucien's hands drifted to her stomach.

"The baby kicked for the first time today," Helena said.

His breath caught in his throat, his entire body going still. Slowly, he sank to his knees, caressing her rounded stomach. He pressed his ear against her skirts and whispered, "You should be kind to your mother."

Helena laughed and curled her fingers in his hair as he kissed her stomach. "Do you hope that we have a son?" she asked. "Will you be disappointed if it is a daughter?"

He shook his head and gazed up at her. Helena watched him in turn, her face softened with affection. "I want whatever child you see fit to give me," Lucien said. "Whether that is a boy or a girl. I will consider myself fortunate simply to have a child by you, one who will grow to be as clever and brilliant as you."

Helena stroked his hair. "You are too good to me."

"It is long past time for someone to be good to you." He paused, considering. "I learned something when I was in London, and I have been trying to find some way to tell you about it."

"Oh?" Helena asked.

He nodded slowly. "I received news of Sir Bertram. It seems as if he has decided to spend some time abroad."

Helena blinked, looking taken aback. "I see."

"It has been a deservedly difficult year for the man," Lucien said. "The *ton* has agreed that you were a victim of his schemes, and you have only drawn their admiration by continuing despite his efforts. It seems as though we may finally put the matter entirely behind us."

Helena laughed. "I thought we already had."

"Perhaps," he said, climbing to his feet. "But I know that Sir Bertram has haunted you still, for all these months. You have said little about him, but I... I know, my sweet."

"You know me too well," she said.

"I should know you quite well," Lucien said. "After all, we have lived together for a long time. It would be stranger if I had not noticed."

Helena gazed at him with an expression that seemed both intense and soft all at once. It was as if she could not quite believe that they were really married and that she would have his love for ever.

"You are right," Helena said, sighing. "I did not realise how much I had become accustomed to being afraid. Even after your performance at Mrs Langley's ball, I worried that Sir Bertram might resume his scheming against me. It is not a constant fear, but I have thought on occasion that he might return without warning and tear my world apart."

Lucien clenched his jaw. "He will not," he said. "Even if he did return, I would ensure that he would never cause you any harm."

"I know that," Helena said.

He rubbed circles over her upper back. She leaned into his touch with a contented sigh. Lucien held her for a long moment, just enjoying how her familiar body felt against his own.

"All you have to worry about is getting sufficient rest and finishing your manuscript," Lucien said. "I will handle the rest."

Helena wrapped her arms around his neck and drew him in for another kiss. He pressed his lips hard against hers, trying to express with that one romantic gesture just how much he loved her. A low groan came from her throat as her fingers tangled in his hair.

"You are so perfect," he murmured, breaking the kiss.

"Perfect for you," she said.

"Yes. Now, shall I escort you to your bed?" Lucien asked. "You do need to rest."

Helena smiled. "I might let you lead me to bed now."

Lucien offered his arm. Helena placed her hand at the crook of his arm and pressed her cheek against his shoulder.

"I do want to argue with you," Helena said. "However, I will concede that I am a little tired."

"Were you too tired to find your boots?" he asked, amused.

"No," she said. "I want to feel the grass beneath my feet."

"I see. Shall I try, also?"

He halted, grinning. Helena laughed as Lucien removed his boots. He floundered a little, struggling to keep his balance. The grass beneath his feet was soft and faintly damp. He flexed his toes, lips twitching in amusement. "The staff will think we are mad," he said, "walking about without our boots."

Helena laughed. "I am certain that they have seen stranger behaviour from us."

"That may be true."

He abandoned his boots along the path and walked alongside her. The ground was strange against his bare feet, in some places harsh and in others swept with grass softer than anything he had ever felt before. Helena seemed unbothered by it. His gaze kept drifting to her, utterly unruffled.

"Did you often walk about like this when your father was alive?" Lucien asked.

She cast him a puzzled look. "Why do you ask?"

"Your eccentricities," he said kindly. "I wonder if he also liked to feel the ground beneath his feet."

"Sometimes," she said. "Do you?"

"Not yet." Lucien flashed her a smile. "But perhaps I will learn. For you, I shall certainly try."

When they entered the house, all was quiet. Lucien pulled the door closed behind them.

"It seems as though Langford and Beatrice have finally retired," Lucien said.

"Were they still speaking when you came to speak with me?" Helena asked, arching an eyebrow. "When I went into the conservatory, I heard them speaking to one another, so they must have been speaking to one another for quite some time."

"I find it difficult to believe that they have anything left to learn about the other," Lucien said slyly.

Helena playfully swatted at his arm. "Leave them be! I think Langford is well-suited for Beatrice."

Lucien let her take the lead up the stairs. Helena had not yet shown any difficulty in moving about Ravensgrave, but he could not deny that a little jolt of anxiety went through him when she engaged in anything strenuous. He would not be a man who treated her like glass, but he would ensure that he was close behind her if she needed him.

"He has likely not mentioned it to you," Lucien said, "but Langford enjoys reading novels. I imagine that he finds Beatrice's discussions about literature to be invigorating."

"Really?"

"Yes," Lucien said. "We shall see if that fondness for literature blooms into something larger."

"Would you be displeased with that?" Helena asked, arching an eyebrow.

"Not in the least," Lucien said. "Given the woman I married, I do not feel as if I can judge whom my cousin chooses."

They reached the door to her bedchamber, and Helena clasped her hands behind her back, smiling coyly at him. "Would you care to join me? I know that we can have no amorous congress, but I would not refuse you if you wished to simply lie beside me."

"I would never deny you that," Lucien said.

He opened the door and bowed cordially to her. With a grin, Helena curtsied. Lucien closed the door behind them and followed Helena as she crossed the room. She threw her coat onto the nearby chair and stood before him in her chemise and stays, the white material sweeping over her delicate form.

"Beautiful," he said.

Helena turned and sat back on the bed. "Thank you," she said. "I am glad that you still find me beautiful after all this time."

He drew her in for another kiss, gentle and intimate. Then Lucien settled onto his side and propped himself up on his elbow, watching his wife. She was his, and he was hers.

Forever.

THE END

Also by Sienna Devereaux

Thank you for indulging in "**The Ruinous Duke's Desire**"!

I hope it left you blushing and breathless! If you're tempted, come lose yourself in another sinful tale in **my full Amazon Book Catalogue here:**

https://go.siennadevereaux.com/bc-authorpage

Thank you for being the reason I get to turn passion into pages! ♥ □

Made in the USA
Monee, IL
17 October 2025

32299919R00142